'I told you ... said, his voice

Her eyes flickered to his mouth and back to his chocolate gaze. 'I..,I can't do that.' She swallowed. 'I just can't.' She licked her bone-dry lips, fighting for time. 'Please, I need to write this book and I need it to sell. I can't survive without it. I have commitments, a mortgage—'

'Withdraw the book proposal and I'll see to your commitments. I'll settle all your debts.'

'You can't be serious?' She stared at him incredulously. 'Surely there must be some kind of catch?'

'There is.' He paused.

She held her breath, somehow knowing instinctively that she wasn't going to like this. She was right.

'I want you to marry me.'

**Please join us in welcoming
a talented new author
to the Modern Romance™ series.**

**Melanie Milburne is a fantastic storyteller
with an intense, passionate style!**

Melanie Milburne says: 'I am married to a surgeon, Steve, and have two gorgeous sons, Paul and Phil. I live in Hobart, Tasmania, where I enjoy an active life as a long-distance runner and nationally ranked top ten Master's swimmer. I also have a Master's Degree in Education, but my children totally turned me off the idea of teaching! When not running or swimming, I write, and when I'm not doing all of the above I'm reading. And if someone could invent a way for me to read during a four-kilometre swim I'd be even happier!'

HIS INCONVENIENT WIFE

BY
MELANIE MILBURNE

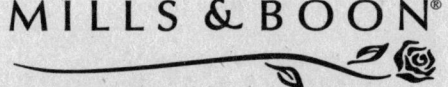

To Phyll Meikle and Ina Shepherd,
the Fairy Godmothers

DID YOU PURCHASE THIS BOOK WITHOUT A COVER?

If you did, you should be aware it is **stolen property** as it was reported *unsold and destroyed* by a retailer. Neither the author nor the publisher has received any payment for this book.

All the characters in this book have no existence outside the imagination of the author, and have no relation whatsoever to anyone bearing the same name or names. They are not even distantly inspired by any individual known or unknown to the author, and all the incidents are pure invention.

All Rights Reserved including the right of reproduction in whole or in part in any form. This edition is published by arrangement with Harlequin Enterprises II B.V. The text of this publication or any part thereof may not be reproduced or transmitted in any form or by any means, electronic or mechanical, including photocopying, recording, storage in an information retrieval system, or otherwise, without the written permission of the publisher.

This book is sold subject to the condition that it shall not, by way of trade or otherwise, be lent, resold, hired out or otherwise circulated without the prior consent of the publisher in any form of binding or cover other than that in which it is published and without a similar condition including this condition being imposed on the subsequent purchaser.

MILLS & BOON and MILLS & BOON with the Rose Device are registered trademarks of the publisher.

First published in Great Britain 2003
Harlequin Mills & Boon Limited,
Eton House, 18-24 Paradise Road, Richmond, Surrey TW9 1SR

© Melanie Milburne 2003

ISBN 0 263 83709 2

Set in Times Roman 10½ on 11 pt.
01-0104-52106

Printed and bound in Spain
by Litografia Rosés, S.A., Barcelona

CHAPTER ONE

SHE hated it when he was late.

Emily checked her watch for the fifteenth time and sighed. Why couldn't Danny be on time for once? The doorbell sounded and she flew to her feet, swiftly checking her reflection in the hall mirror as she rushed past. Taking two deep, calming breaths, she opened the door with a big welcoming smile plastered on her mouth.

'You?' She stared at Danny's older brother in shock. 'What are you doing here?'

Damien Margate's dark eyes swept over her red cocktail dress and back to her face before he responded coolly, 'Danny can't make it. I've come in his place.'

Emily's mouth dropped open and a fluttering feeling of panic stirred deep in her stomach.

'He's...he's not...hurt or something, is he?'

Damien shook his head as he moved past her and into her tiny flat.

'Not yet,' he said with a cryptic edge to his voice.

Emily's eyes flew to his, her expression guarded.

'But I don't understand. Danny knows how important tonight is to me. Why hasn't he phoned and told me himself he can't make it?'

Damien shrugged in that detestably aloof way that had annoyed her the first time she'd met him.

'Like you, I am not always party to my younger brother's intentions. I realise how insulting it must be to you to have to tolerate my presence instead of his, but as I'm here now you can make up your own mind about whether you wish to be accompanied by me.'

She opened and closed her mouth, not trusting herself to

speak. Her eyes travelled over his tall figure, imposing in the black dinner suit, his classic bow-tie perfectly symmetrical with his collar points. Danny would've still been tying his as he rang the doorbell. But then, Danny was nothing like Damien.

'I wouldn't like to take up your valuable time,' she began with an attempt at sarcasm. 'I'm sure you've got much better things to do than escort me to a literary awards night.'

'On the contrary.' His eyes travelled to hers, their dark depths unreadable. 'I had nothing better to do...this evening.'

Emily felt herself seething. How dare he come here and ridicule her? He knew how much she hated him, especially since he'd expressed his views on her proposed biography of his and Danny's aunt, Rose. He'd accused her of ingratiating herself into the family in order to fabricate a parcel of lies about an old lady who could no longer defend herself.

'No hot date tonight?' Emily's mouth curved into a mocking smile as she added, 'Or did she decide to spend the evening with her husband after all?'

She knew she shouldn't have said it almost the second the words had left her lips. His eyes hardened, their dark chocolate depths glittering with suppressed anger.

'I take it Danny's been filling your head with nonsense again?' His tone gave nothing away but Emily could sense his usual iron-clad control was wavering. Knowing she'd been able to rattle his cage even slightly made her feel powerful, something she wasn't used to feeling around Damien Margate.

'I didn't realise it was a family secret,' she said recklessly. 'At least not another one.'

He closed the gap between them in one stride, one of his hands taking her slim wrist in a gentle but firm hold. She had to crane her neck to get eye contact; he was a good four inches taller than his brother's six feet and it made her feel intimidated, which, she was certain, had been his intention.

'A word of advice, Miss Sherwood.' He spoke evenly but a threat lurked behind the words. 'You might have plans to write a book about a relative of mine, but that doesn't give you free rein to speculate on my personal life, either publicly or privately. Is that understood?'

She tried to out-stare him but it was impossible. Her eyes flickered to the knot of his bow-tie and then back to his firm, disapproving mouth.

'I'm not the slightest bit interested in your private life,' she said through clenched teeth. 'If indeed you have one. Now, please let me go.'

His hold on her wrist tightened just a fraction to counter her attempt to pull away.

'The way I see it, you have two choices. You can go to this cocktail party on your own, which will set tongues wagging on why you're not being partnered, or you can come with me. What's it to be?'

'The tongues will certainly wag if I turn up with you,' she pointed out. 'Danny is my boyfriend, not you.'

'Danny is unavailable this evening,' he reminded her. 'Won't being partnered by me authenticate your plans to document my aunt's life?'

She wished she could throw his offer in his face but he was right. A member of the family being present would be noted by the press and that in itself would give some sort of credibility to her book. If she went alone it could easily add to the speculation that she'd already alienated the Margate family. One whiff of a problem and her publishers would pull the plug.

She needed this next book to sell. Her agent was temperamental at the best of times, and since her last biography had floundered ignominiously she really had no choice. But why couldn't it have been Danny who escorted her? After all, they were known to be an item and that would surely lift her profile.

'Well?' Damien's hand on her arm felt like a rope burn. She could feel her skin prickling in reaction to his flesh on hers.

'It seems I have very little choice in the matter.' Her voice was tight with resentment.

He let her arm go but his eyes still held hers.

'It matters little either way to me, but I would guess this evening is of paramount importance to you. Isn't that correct?'

She'd been nominated for a small award, along with two other biographers. Promotion, particularly self-promotion, wasn't her thing but her agent had insisted.

'I need the advance buzz. This is going to be an important book,' she said somewhat breathlessly. 'People want to know about the private lives of celebrities.'

'They deserve to know the truth,' he said, 'not some fabricated fairy story guaranteed to boost sales.'

Emily gave him a challenging look.

'Why should you care? I'm not planning to write anything about you.'

'I can assure you, Miss Sherwood, that if you so much as write a single word about me you'll personally answer to the consequences.'

'Oh?' She gave him a scathing look. 'Is that supposed to frighten me? If so, I'm afraid it won't be successful. I plan to write a book about your aunt and nothing you say is going to stop me.'

'Don't say I didn't warn you.' His eyes glittered dangerously. 'You might have wrapped my younger brother around one of those quick-typing little fingers of yours but I'm another story entirely.'

Something about him made her uneasy. She hadn't felt so reprimanded since high school, when she'd forgotten to bring her gym gear to class. Damn him for making her feel so childish and irresponsible. She'd show him! Let him do his worst—tonight was her chance to haul herself out of financial ruin and nothing he could say or do was going to stop her.

She schooled her features into a guileless smile.

'I understand perfectly, Mr Margate. I am very honoured that you've seen fit to accompany me to this cocktail party in place of your brother. I'll just get my wrap and we can get going.'

She flounced away to snatch up her purse and wrap, a victorious little smile hovering around her mouth. He might think he could threaten her with his diamond-sharp gaze but she still held the upper hand. There were things about him he had no idea she knew. It gave her a much needed boost of confidence to imagine his reaction when she finally dished the dirt on him and the rest of his family.

The cocktail party was in full swing when they arrived. Emily's agent, Clarice Connor, came towards them, a vision in voluminous carmine chiffon, a glass of champagne raised in a toast.

'Darling! How fashionably late you are.' She air-kissed Emily's smooth cheeks before eyeing Damien up and down. 'My, my, my,' she drooled, 'the older brother instead. How clever of you, Emily.'

'I don't believe we've met.' Damien extended a hand, his expression shuttered.

Clarice took his hand, clasping it towards her ample bosom. 'The pleasure's all mine. How wonderful that you could come tonight.' She turned to Emily. 'Where's the boy?'

Emily's mouth tightened when she saw the sardonic gleam in Damien's eyes at Clarice's words.

'He's—'

'He sends his apologies,' Damien cut in before Emily could think of something to say. 'Something important cropped up.'

'Well—' Clarice waved a careless taloned hand '—he's served his purpose, hasn't he, my love?'

Emily felt her cheeks storm with colour.

'But how nice that you could make it.' Clarice simpered at Damien. 'I mean, with your busy social schedule and all.'

Damien gave her a slight nod.

'I'm sure this evening will be very worthwhile,' he said with a cool smile.

'Indeed.' Clarice turned towards Emily. 'There's a journo from the *Melbourne Age* who wants to interview you. I've spoken to him about making an appointment but he insists on speaking to you this evening. I think you should do what you can to promote this new project as much as possible, even if it means mixing with people you wouldn't normally mix with.' At that she gave Damien a meaningful look, but he had already turned to speak to someone who'd just arrived.

Emily watched as the elegant woman approached him, her clinging black dress outlining her stunning curves as she walked across the floor.

'Damien! How lovely to see you.'

Something in Damien's face must have warned the woman of the presence of Emily. She gave Emily an all-encompassing look.

'Hello. Are you someone important?'

Emily didn't know quite what to make of the woman's greeting. She flicked a glance at Damien but his face, as usual, was impassive.

'Nerolie, this is Emily Sherwood,' Damien said. 'Miss Sherwood, this is Nerolie Highstock.'

Nerolie's eyes didn't quite reflect the smile that hovered about her thin lips. 'Oh, are you a writer as well? I'm afraid I'd never heard of you until this evening.'

As insults went it was well aimed. Emily knew she didn't qualify for the Booker Prize, but her first book had been well received and moderately successful even if her last hadn't quite made the top ten. Nerolie enjoyed the top ten status her only book had achieved with prima donna fastidiousness. Emily wasn't one to criticise her success, even if she privately thought it had been a matter of being in the right place at the right time, which in Nerolie's case had been her agent's bed.

'I suppose that depends on the genre one reads,' Emily said cuttingly.

Nerolie chose to ignore that and turned to Damien.

'I suppose you're here to make sure Miss Sherwood behaves herself? I've heard she was quite ruthless with the skeletons in the previous closets she's raided.'

'So—' Emily met the other woman's cold eyes with a flash of fire in her own '—you have read my other books? I thought you hadn't heard of me before?'

Nerolie gave her a sweeping glance.

'I'm afraid, Miss Sherwood, I have no time for the money-making mud-raking that constitutes most of today's unauthorised biographies. I prefer fact to fiction every time.'

'And how do you decide just what is fact and what is fiction?' Emily queried.

Nerolie Highstock's cold grey eyes hardened. 'I've always believed in getting things straight from the horse's mouth.'

'And what if the horse refuses to speak?' Emily asked, flicking a glance towards the tall, silent figure between them.

Nerolie's thin mouth tightened before she responded chillingly, 'I'm sure there are some horses that are best left alone. You'd do well to acknowledge that, Miss Sherwood, before one of them kicks you in retaliation.' With that parting shot she swung away to speak to another guest, and Emily smiled a self-satisfied little cat's smile.

'Miaow,' Damien breathed just near her left shoulder.

She felt the warm brush of his breath on her bare skin and shivered in reaction. She stepped away from him, glaring up at his mocking expression.

'I wasn't aware you were on intimate terms with the likes

of Ms Highstock. What a pity she doesn't have a husband to make the chase all the more alluring.'

The fire in his eyes could have burned her if it hadn't been for the timely arrival of the guest of honour. The chief editor of the publishing house tapped the microphone as a prelude to his speech and all eyes turned towards the small podium.

Emily felt the steely presence of Damien Margate at her back. He wasn't quite touching her, but she knew if she moved even a fraction backwards she would encounter his rock-hard frame. As if under the influence of a magnetic field, all the way through the loquacious speech Emily felt her body threatening to betray her by rocking backwards to touch him. She had to will herself to stand perfectly still— every muscle tense, every nerve under tight control just in case she gave in to the temptation.

She was concentrating so hard she missed her name. She suddenly became aware of everyone's eyes on her and, stumbling forward, approached the podium. She knew she'd been nominated for the award for her first book, but had put any thought of success out of her mind after the collapse of her second. The small award presented to her totally surprised her.

Afterwards, she couldn't quite recall what she had said. She knew she'd thanked Clarice and her two editors, but apart from that it was all a blur. Her mouth spoke, words spilling out in a more or less educated and articulate order, but all the while she felt the cold hard stare of Damien Margate, which made her palms resting on the lectern moisten as she gripped its edges for support.

Several people swarmed around her afterwards for autographs and she was grateful for the reprieve. She wasn't looking forward to the drive home, feeling sure there would be hell to pay for her reckless taunts earlier.

She didn't know what had come over her tonight. It really was none of her business what Damien got up to in his private life. His aloof carriage was an attraction for her, she conceded privately, but only because she was a writer and such guarded subjects held a certain appeal. It was absolutely nothing to do with him personally. He didn't even have the boy-next-door good looks which caused her to gravitate towards Danny. Danny's playboy blue eyes and fly-away blond curls were what she went for, not the dark and brooding, too-tall-to-kiss features of someone like Damien.

She cast a covert glance towards him across the crowded room and was startled to see him looking at her. She felt her cheeks grow warm, turned to the next person waiting for her autograph in the queue and distractedly scribbled something on the flyleaf of her first book.

Eventually the evening came to a close and Emily had no choice but to face Damien, who was waiting to one side as the last of the guests farewelled her.

'Thank you for coming.' Emily smiled, shaking the last of the hands.

Clarice had already made her way out, and short of handing out freebies to the catering staff Emily had no choice but to pick up her evening purse and join Damien.

'Ready?' He looked down at her flushed features, a satirical smile lurking about his firm mouth.

'I...yes.' She gathered her wrap around her shoulders. 'But I can easily get a cab. I wouldn't want to interrupt any of your plans for the rest of the evening.'

'You seem in rather a hurry to get rid of me,' he observed. 'I would've thought you'd relish the opportunity to milk the situation for all it's worth.'

A frown of puzzlement settled between her brows and he continued, 'You could conduct your own private interview with me. Who knows what you might find out to put in your next book?'

Emily shifted her eyes from the piercing laser of his.

'I have no wish to interview you, or indeed spend any more time with you than is absolutely necessary out of common politeness. Now, if you'll excuse me, I need to use the bathroom. I'll meet you in the foyer in...five minutes.' She swung away, her head high, and walked stiffly towards the conveniences.

Her exit was only slightly spoilt by her cannoning into an elderly gentleman coming out of the male toilet on her own way in. Emily bolted inside the correct door, her colour high.

She stood in front of the gilt-edged mirror and took some calming breaths. Her hair was tumbling out of its restraint on top of her head, falling in curly tendrils around her cheeks. Her blue eyes looked wide, the dark pupils dilated, the lashes fluttering as if in panic.

She washed the dampness off her hands and quickly made her way out of the bathroom. Instead of heading for the foyer she turned towards the nearest fire escape and tiptoed down the echoing stairs to freedom.

The night had cooled somewhat and the street was packed with crowds spilling out of Sydney's theatres and cinemas. Emily joined the bustling throng and made her way towards a small café three blocks away, which she and Danny had been to many times. She pushed open the glass doors and scanned the room for a quiet corner in which to gather herself until she felt it was safe to go home without running into Damien.

Her eyes came to rest on a fly-away blond head in the left corner. It was bending towards a bright red-gold female head, hands entwined intimately on the table between them.

Her breath caught in her throat and her stomach clenched in shock. Just then a large hand settled on her shoulder and she felt the warm presence of Damien Margate brush her body from behind.

'My car's just outside if you'd still like a lift.'

Emily turned past his broad shoulder and stumbled blindly from the café. She pushed herself through the clots of people, almost turning her ankle as she tripped on a discarded beer can.

She felt him grasp her elbow. She didn't pull away, and

his fingers slid down her arm and took her hand into the strength of his.

'Come on.' He gave her hand a little tug. 'This way—my car is down here.'

She followed him silently, her hand still captured in his, her mind tumbling with images of Danny and her replacement sitting together at the very table where she'd sat with him, discussing their plans for the future.

A single tear escaped before she could stop it and she brushed it away viciously. Damien flicked her a glance before unlocking his car.

'Come on, get in. I have something I wish to say to you.'

Emily got in without a word. Shock and dismay still pumped through her veins, as well as a deep resentment that Damien Margate of all people was sole witness to it.

CHAPTER TWO

EMILY didn't realise till it was too late that he'd not taken the route to her apartment. Instead he had turned the car towards Double Bay and pulled in before an imposing house of mansion-like proportions.

'I want to go home,' she said in a petulant tone.

'I'll take you home when I've finished with you.'

Emily wasn't sure she liked the ominous edge to his words. What could he possibly want to say to her? A flutter of panic flapped in her stomach like the wings of a startled bird. Surely he didn't intend to hurt her? She glanced at him covertly and tried to reassure herself. She'd interviewed dangerous criminals whilst researching her second book, through the grille of a prison cubicle with armed guards beside her. Who was going to come to her aid if Damien Margate had something sinister planned?

She followed him mutinously into the large house, her eyes widening at the opulent marble in the foyer as he opened the front door. Inside, a bronze statue of a young Rose held pride of place, the subtle down-lighting casting her beautiful features in relief. Emily stood transfixed, her fingers aching to reach out and touch the classic lines of the exquisite face.

'She was only nineteen when she posed for that,' Damien said from just behind her left shoulder.

'She...she's beautiful,' Emily breathed. 'Who's the sculptor?'

He moved towards one of the formal rooms, signalling for her to follow him.

'No one you'd know.'

'Try me,' she said, intrigued.

He shook his head.

'It was never meant to be a public piece so there's no point telling. He's long dead, and Rose—' he shrugged himself out of his dinner suit jacket '—Rose isn't around to give her permission.'

'Where is she?' Emily asked, already knowing his answer. 'Danny insisted he didn't know but surely you do?'

His eyes held hers for a long moment.

'Rose is where people like you cannot harm her, and for as long as I have breath that's where she'll stay.'

'But that's hardly fair on her adoring public,' Emily pointed out. 'The mystery surrounding her disappearance from public life has intensified speculation. All you'd have to do is release a statement about her whereabouts and people would leave her alone.'

His face clouded with anger as he loosened his tie and flung it towards his jacket over the back of one of the plush leather sofas.

'I've seen what the public do to people they no longer have any use for,' he said. 'Anyway, why should I give you the privilege of that information? You'd have it in the press within minutes and a hefty cheque in your bank account to follow. I've seen how you work. What you don't know you make up and the public fall for it.'

'I wasn't aware you took such an active interest in my work.'

'I'm not interested. I just know how people like you operate. That's what this little interlude with Danny was all about, wasn't it?'

'What?' She stared at him.

He gave a harsh laugh.

'Don't bother pretending to be broken-hearted over his defection. No doubt you've milked him dry for all the inside information. Now you've got what you need for your book it shouldn't take all that long to get over him.'

Emily's face drained of colour. 'Danny and I were—'

'Did you sleep with him?' he asked baldly.

'That's none of your business.'

He shrugged carelessly. 'I was just wondering how far someone like you would go. I assume you'd stop at nothing to get what you want.'

'You're disgusting,' she spat.

He gave her a wry look. 'But you picked the wrong brother, didn't you?'

Emily clenched her fists by her sides and wished she had the courage to slap his face.

'I mean you should have worked on me instead. I'm Rose's power of attorney, not Danny. He knows nothing of Rose's affairs.'

'I wouldn't lower myself—' She left the rest of the sentence hanging, her derisive expression filling in the rest.

He gave a harsh laugh as he reached for the door of the drinks cabinet in the wall unit. 'Danny was playing with you just as much as you were playing with him. You both got what you deserved.'

'So where do you fit in?' she asked. 'Why the Sir Galahad routine tonight? Or did you want to witness my fall from grace?'

He poured two measures of brandy into two glasses and handed her one before he spoke.

'Danny is a coward when it comes to confrontation. As for me—' he raised his glass towards her '—I love a fight.'

Emily felt like throwing the brandy in his face and had to tighten her fingers around the glass to stop herself from doing so.

'All the same, I bet you enjoyed it.' She flashed him a malevolent glare. 'In fact, you couldn't have planned it better.'

'I had no idea he was going to be in that café tonight.'

'Didn't you?' she accused.

'I'm not so callous as to rub your nose in it like that, whatever you might think of me. Danny called me and asked if I'd fill in for him tonight—end of story.'

'How magnanimous of you!' She gave him a withering look. 'Tell me, what else did he ask you to do for him?'

'I do have some limits.' He reached for his glass. 'Sleeping with the enemy is one of them.'

She almost choked on her brandy. 'As if I'd let you!'

His eyes ran over her speculatively as he twirled his glass.

'You'd do anything for a story, isn't that how it goes?'

'Not quite anything.'

He laughed and sipped at his brandy.

'You look like some Victorian virgin, compromised by the head of the household, but you're hardly that, are you? I've heard about your little affair with the subject of your first book. It didn't quite pay dividends, though, did it? Although perhaps tonight's award is some sort of late compensation.'

'You can't believe everything you read in the press,' she said, taking a huge gulp of brandy.

'Oh?' His dark brows lifted. 'What happened? Did he get sick of sharing a bed with a notebook? I can imagine it must be quite off-putting to be cornered with an interview pad in one's more intimate moments.'

'Better than being cornered by one's partner's husband,' she put in.

His glass clinked on to the surface of the table with a sharp snap.

'You're very determined to spar with me, aren't you? But I wonder if you have what it really takes?'

'Try me,' she challenged. 'I can give as good as I get.'

'That remains to be seen.'

She sipped at her brandy, her eyes averted.

'You're very close to Rose, aren't you?' she asked after a long pause.

'You'll have to try a little harder with me if you want information.' He gave his glass another twirl.

'I wouldn't waste my time. You haven't got anything I want anyway.'

'You seem very sure of that,' he commented.

'What are you offering?'

'What do you want?'

She took another careful sip of her drink before responding.

'I'd like to know why Rose disappeared from public life.'

'I thought it was common knowledge she's become an alcoholic recluse,' he said evenly.

Emily bit her lip. Danny had told her that story was true. She hadn't made up her mind yet whether to assert it as a fact, but she knew if her agent got wind of it she'd insist on releasing it. It was sure to boost sales, and sales were what she needed most.

'I have it on good authority,' she began uncertainly.

'You picked the wrong authority,' he said. 'I've already consulted my legal representatives. That's what I wanted to discuss with you tonight.'

Emily's eyes widened in alarm. She could tell by the look on his face that something of great import was coming.

'I want you to withdraw your plans to write the book.'

She stared at him in shock.

'You...you can't be serious!' She plonked her barely touched drink on to the nearest surface, uncaring that some of it spilled over the sides and dribbled towards the cream carpet.

'Write it and be sued—your choice.'

She swallowed the bile of fear in her throat.

'So this is why you escorted me tonight?' she threw at him venomously. 'It wasn't to protect me from your brother's perfidy—it was to deliver your own fatal blow.'

Damien put his own drink aside and faced her. 'I don't wish to personally harm you in any way,' he said, 'but I must insist on protecting my family at all costs.'

'So destroying my writing career doesn't come into it at all?'

He hesitated over his reply.

'There are always casualties in these types of situations. It's nothing personal.'

'Don't make me laugh!' she scoffed at him. 'You're intent on bringing me down, aren't you?'

'Nothing could be further from the truth. In fact, I feel rather sorry for you.'

'Whatever for?'

'You're a pawn in the game. People like you are always the ones who lose in the end.'

Emily's eyes flashed with the fire of resentment. 'Please enlighten me. I'm sure you're absolutely dying to anyway.'

He gave another of those could-mean-anything shrugs.

'You're under the thumb of your agent and editors. It's my guess that half the time you're writing what they want, not what you really want to write at all.'

Emily suddenly felt exposed, vulnerable.

'Don't be ridiculous,' she said off-handedly. 'I write what the public wants to read.'

'Lies? Conjecture?'

'No. The truth.'

He gave a rough snort of disbelief as he reached again for his drink.

'You're as deluded as the public who read you. You wouldn't recognise the truth if it laid itself out in front of you.'

'OK, then,' she challenged. 'Tell me the truth. Why has Rose disappeared from public life? If you're such an advocate for the truth then enlighten me.'

'What? And have you fund your pension by revealing the private arrangements of an old lady who no longer wishes to be in the public eye?'

'She was in the public eye for over thirty-five years. Surely that counts for something?'

'No. Not if she doesn't desire it,' he said. 'Celebrities are not public property unless they give their permission to be so. Rose decided that enough was enough and the rest of her years should be spent in seclusion. I respect that and so should you.'

'But why all the secrecy?' Emily asked. 'Lots of celebrities quietly retreat from public life without question. Rose's sudden departure has fuelled the public's interest. One statement from you and I could tie up all the loose ends and she could live the rest of her life in peace.'

'You never give up, do you?' He eyeballed her over the rim of his brandy glass. 'Always on the hunt for information, always the investigative journalist.'

Emily reclaimed her glass and took a tentative sip. She didn't drink brandy as a rule, but didn't want to appear unsophisticated in his company.

'I'm committed to providing the public with what they want.'

'Even if you hurt innocent people in the process?'

Emily bit her lip once more. She was still haunted by the images of the parents of the target of her previous book. They'd pleaded with her to represent him differently but she'd had to follow her agent's directions.

'I do what I'm told to do.'

'Well, I'm telling you to halt the book. Write something else. Anything but a book about my aunt.'

'I can't do that. That award I received will ensure my success. My agent is already pushing for a contract from my publisher.'

He reached for his jacket, which was lying across the sofa.

'How much?' he asked, fanning open the leather pouch of his wallet. 'I can cover your losses. How much?'

Emily felt sick, cheapened by his implied insult.

'You couldn't afford me,' she stated in a flat tone.

One of his dark brows lifted.

'I could cover your costs and set you up for a new book. Something a little less controversial.'

'Controversy sells,' she said. 'I need sales or my career is over.'

'How much?' he asked again, brandishing his wallet.

Emily gave him a scornful look. 'Is that what you say to all the girls?'

His expression clouded. 'I'm making you a generous offer—take it or leave it.'

'I'll leave it,' she said arrogantly. 'I've got a lot riding on the release of this new book.'

'You're willing to risk everything for it?' he asked.

'Do your worst, Mr Margate.' She glared at him. 'I'm not frightened of you.'

'You should be,' he warned. 'I have the means to totally destroy your literary career.'

'I'm increasingly fascinated as to why you would want to,' she said archly. 'It seems to me you're very threatened by the exposure my proposed book represents. It makes me start to wonder exactly what it is you're so protective of. According to my sources, you and Danny have had very little to do with Rose over the last fifteen years. I can't help wondering why you'd be so motivated to protect her now.'

'Tell me, Miss Sherwood.' His eyes held hers with determination. 'Do you come from a close family?'

Emily lowered her gaze and concentrated on the amber fluid in her glass. 'I have two siblings. My parents died some years ago.'

'I'm sorry.'

She looked up at him. There was a sincerity about his simple comment that touched her unexpectedly.

'It's OK,' she said dismissively. 'My...family have never been close. My parents divorced when I was four. I'm used to being alone.'

Damien perched on the edge of one of the leather sofas and cupped his brandy balloon in one large hand.

'Is that why you've chosen to write biographies?'

'What do you mean?'

He twirled the glass in his hand reflectively.

'Writing about other people's families must answer some sort of need of your own, surely?'

She decided against responding to his comments and instead wandered out of his line of vision to inspect the walnut bookcase. He was certainly an eclectic reader, she observed, but there was no sign of an Emily Sherwood title. The tinge of pique she experienced was both unexpected and unsettling.

'Isn't that why you delve into other people's private lives? To make up for the close family you didn't have yourself?' he added.

'I find people's lives interesting.' She turned to face him again. 'Even those who aren't famous in any way. It has nothing to do with me personally. Besides—' she gave him a provocative look '—it's about making money—lots of money.'

'You callous little bitch,' he snarled, tossing his wallet on to the coffee table. 'This isn't about money at all. This is about power, isn't it? Danny's unfaithfulness has given you even more reason to hurt the Margate name now, hasn't it?'

Emily tried to outstare him but his eyes were burning with a hatred that frightened her. She drained her brandy and put the empty glass down with a betraying little clatter on to the coffee table next to his abandoned wallet.

'You have a very poor notion of a biographer's life if you think I would spend months of my life researching a book at great personal cost to simply abandon the task just because one of the relatives couldn't keep his fly zipped.'

Damien's eyes narrowed as he stood before her.

'Danny and Louise Morse have been on and off together for months. If you're such a hot-shot investigative journalist you should've picked that up from the outset.'

Emily's face suffused with colour but she maintained her poise. Damien Margate was a formidable opponent but he had a lot to lose. Danny had been a pleasant and entertaining distraction for her—useful too, in providing her with access to family albums and journals. But she hadn't been in love with Danny by any means. She'd been toying with the idea of sleeping with him, however, and that did make her feel very foolish. She didn't usually make those sorts of errors of judgement.

'Perhaps I'm like you,' she taunted him rashly. 'I don't mind sharing.'

He moved quickly, and the sofa behind her blocked her exit so effectively that she suddenly found herself jammed up against his chest, his long strong legs tangling with her shaky ones.

'I seem to remember warning you about making careless statements about my private life.' He glowered down at her. 'But you don't listen to warnings, do you?'

Her voice, when it came out, seemed to be squeezed out of her chest. 'I...I'm not frightened of you.'

'Yes, you are.' One of his fingers lifted her chin to make her meet his diamond-sharp eyes. 'You've got everything resting on this new book, haven't you? And I've got every reason to stop you from writing it.'

'You can't stop me.'

'Oh, can't I?' The light of challenge in his eyes made her stomach free-fall in panic.

'I'll fight you.'

'Go on, then.' He gave a half-grunt of mocking laughter. 'Fight me.'

She ached to scratch his face. Every nerve in her body wanted to claw at him, bring him to his knees, turn the tables on him so it was him begging, not her.

She met his eyes, her breath catching in her throat at his nearness. His face was so close, his eyes burning into hers. Her legs threatened to dissolve beneath her and yet she didn't have either the strength to pull away or the inclination. Part of her wanted to find out just how far he would go. That same part of her wanted to see if she could push him that little bit further...

His mouth found hers, shocking her with its heat and purpose. This wasn't a kiss of experimentation; this was a kiss of premeditated punishment. His firm lips opened over her startled mouth and he entered it with a single thrust of his tongue that sent her rocking backwards, but his strong arms around her gave her no choice but to stay imprinted along the length of his probing and insistent frame.

She should have been fighting him, but instead of her hands pushing him away they grasped at his shirt sleeves, her fingernails embedding in the silky fabric, pulling him even closer to her fevered body.

His tongue duelled with hers moistly. Heat flicked along her veins, ran up her legs and pooled between her thighs where his very male body was imprinting a message older than time.

One of his hands left the back of her head and slipped under the tiny shoestring strap of her cocktail dress. The flimsy ribbon-like strap fell away and the crest of one creamy breast was before his hungry eyes. She could feel the heat of his gaze as his eyes travelled over the smooth, proud mound, the dusky redness of her nipple clearly visible as the strap slipped a little further.

His mouth found the sensitive skin of her neck, his tongue grazing the underside of her jaw, trailing a relentless path back to her waiting mouth.

'No!'

Somehow she found the strength of will to push him from her. She stood in disarray before him—her mouth swollen with his kisses, her breasts burgeoning from his touch, her legs shaking from the heat of his maleness pressing against her so intimately.

'No?' His dark eyes were sardonic, his mouth a thin line of derision.

She had to look away. His satirical gaze made her feel cheap and colour flooded her face.

'I won't tell Danny,' he said insultingly. 'Your secret's safe with me.'

Emily felt sick. The nausea rose like a tide in her stomach. How had she got herself into this situation? Her big night of fame had turned into a farce of mammoth proportions. He'd swiftly manoeuvred the situation so that it was she who was cast in the role of the fool. He was in control, had been from the first, and was now just waiting for an opportunity to dispense with her for good.

'If you think you can manipulate me by such means, think again,' she spat at him. 'I'm well used to the groping hands of desperate men, and I know how to deal with them.'

One dark eyebrow rose expressively. 'I would hardly describe myself as desperate, but please enlighten me all the same.'

'You're just like all the rest.' Her eyes flashed with hatred. 'You think you can snap your fingers and women will come running, but I've got news for you. I know the only women you've had have been other men's cast-offs, and I'm not going to add myself to the list.'

Emily knew she'd gone way too far. The glitter of venom in his dark eyes impaled her to the spot. He was just a breath away, and she flinched as one of his hands circled her wrist and tugged her back into the wall of his chest.

'Not only are the words you write dangerous,' he rasped. 'So are the ones that come out of that delectable mouth of yours. But I'm going to make you regret every one of them.'

'I told you—you don't frighten me,' she gasped as his rock-hard pelvis collided with hers.

'You have one week to come to a decision,' he continued, as if she hadn't spoken. 'If at the end of that week you have failed to withdraw your proposal to write this book, any further dealings we have will be via my lawyers.'

'You can't do that!'

His eyes glinted challengingly. 'Watch me.'

Panic beat a tattoo in her chest. If her publisher got wind of a threatened suit they'd pull the plug immediately, without sparing her a single thought.

She pushed herself away from him and, snatching up her purse and wrap, headed for the door.

'I'll take you home,' he said, reaching for his keys.

She swung around to glare at him.

'I'd rather crawl on my knees than accept a lift from you.' She wrenched open the front door of his house and flung back at him, 'I'll see you in court.'

CHAPTER THREE

EMILY hailed the first cab she could and sat shivering in the back seat, her heart thumping with adrenalin as she recalled Damien Margate's threats. The familiar lights of the city blurred in front of her agitated eyes as she contemplated her next move.

She didn't have the means to fight someone like Damien. Her literary career was already hanging by a thread—her agent, Clarice, had warned her only a few days ago of the importance of the success of this next book.

Emily paid her fare and stood looking up at her tiny apartment as the taxi drove away. She'd worked so hard to have a place to call her own. The success of her first biography about a prominent politician had paid the deposit and furnished it. The failure of her second book had rattled her security somewhat, but she'd clung on with fervent promises to her bank manager as well as a part-time job at a local restaurant.

She dreamed of the day when she could write full-time, but so far that possibility had eluded her. So she scratched at bits of notepaper and tapped at her old lap-top whenever she could, working frantically to deadlines, trying hard to please editors and pandering to Clarice, who claimed to believe in her but often acted as if she couldn't wait to weasel her way out of her contract.

Emily sighed as she waited for the lift. She wouldn't give in without a fight, even if it took every ounce of courage she had. Damien Margate probably thought he could scare her with a few idle threats but she'd show him. She had all weekend to plan her counter-attack.

She slept fitfully, too wound up to relax enough to drop

off. As soon as eight o'clock came around she called Clarice, who answered the phone groggily. 'Yes?'

'Clarice, it's me, Emily. I want to go on tour to promote *Rose's Cupboard*.'

Emily heard the sound of Clarice's bedsprings protesting.

'But you haven't written it yet.'

'So what? I won that award. People will go out and buy my previous titles. I want you to ring around and organise as many book signings as you can for *Going For Vote*. And not just bookshops—I'll do shopping centres, radio shows and breakfast television.'

'I don't believe I'm hearing this,' Clarice said. 'You told me after *Tyson's Trial* you were never going to self-promote again.'

'I know, I know—but this is different.'

'Does the boy know about this?' Clarice asked.

'This has absolutely nothing to do with Danny,' Emily said firmly.

'What about that brother of his? I don't suppose this was his idea?'

'Damien Margate is a stuck-up prig who probably hasn't read anything but the *Financial Times* since high school. I want to promote myself, and nothing and no one is going to stop me.'

'Attagirl!' Clarice cheered. 'Give me a couple of hours—I'll see what I can organise at short notice.'

'Thanks, Clarice,' she said. 'You won't be sorry. I know this one's going to be a hit.'

'Yes, well, it'd better be, my love. We can't afford another disaster like *Tyson's Trial*. That sort of bad publicity is best left for movie stars, not authors and agents.'

Emily hated being reminded of her book about a young offender. When Tyson had committed suicide behind bars it seemed everyone had blamed her, including his distraught family. It had taken her months to even think of writing again, and then only because of a chance encounter with Danny.

He'd come into the restaurant where she worked and as she'd served him he'd chatted to her in a flirting and easy-going manner. When he'd signed his credit card she'd noticed the Margate name. She'd made some comment about the famous stage actress Rose Margate, who had taken the theatre world by storm, only to mysteriously disappear from public view without so much as a departing interview.

'She's my aunt,' he'd said, pocketing his credit card, his light-blue eyes glinting at hers.

Emily had taken up his offer of a late-night drink somewhere. That somewhere had been his plush Northbridge apartment, and that evening had restarted her writing career with a bang.

Clarice Connor had been beside herself once Emily's synopsis landed on her desk. 'An unauthorised biography of Rose Margate? Wonderful, darling! But do you have to sleep with this Boy Wonder to get all the inside info?'

'Not yet—' Emily had laughed '—but it's tempting.'

She hadn't known about Danny's older brother until Damien had come to the restaurant one evening with an elegantly dressed woman on his arm. She'd seen his name in the reservations book and was too much of a journalist not to notice the gold wedding band almost embedded into the flesh of his date's left ring finger. Danny had told her of his brother's affair with a prominent businessman's wife but he'd insisted on her not mentioning anything to do with his brother in her book. Emily had been intrigued, of course, but after a while had taken it to mean that Danny was just being protective.

Rose's Cupboard had proved to be much harder to research than she'd expected. Danny had been generous, handing her various letters and photo albums and two dog-eared childhood journals. The library had provided numerous paper clippings, and several theatres had shown her through their archives, where Rose's beautiful face adorned many a promotional poster. But, while Emily had been able to piece together Rose's early years and much of her performing years, there were still yawning gaps that made the task of documenting her life extremely difficult.

She'd probed Danny for relatives and friends to interview, but it seemed the Margate family didn't have many close friends and what relatives there were, such as Damien, were very tight-lipped.

At last she had decided to approach Damien Margate one more time. He was, after all, Rose's power of attorney. Perhaps he might come to agree with her that Rose's adoring fans genuinely deserved to know what had become of her.

Emily had made an appointment at his office and sat fidgeting in his plush waiting room for over an hour. Somehow she'd known the delay was deliberate.

When he'd finally summoned her into his office she had had to fight to keep her temper under control. Irritated with having to wait, annoyed at being treated like a persistent fly, she had plastered a determined smile on her face and taken the seat he'd offered on the other side of his desk.

'What can I do for you, Miss Sherwood?' he drawled, ignoring his own chair to remain standing behind the expanse of his desk. 'Are you after some financial advice?'

Emily worked even harder on her smile, resenting him even more for not sitting down and giving her craning neck a rest.

'I was hoping we could have a talk about your aunt—'

'No.' His single word was delivered both adamantly and sharply.

Emily took a calming breath and tried again. 'But what if you were the main collaborator on the biography?' she asked. 'I'd only write what you wanted me to write. You'd have total control.'

Damien's hawk-like eyes pierced her blue gaze.

'I told you before, I have no intention of revealing information about my aunt to anyone, and most particularly not to you.'

Emily clenched her hands in her lap, desperately fighting the desire to slam them down on his desk in frustration. She was certain he could tell she was losing her cool and it made her all the more determined not to do so. All the same, her nails had imprinted themselves in her palms by the time she trusted herself to speak once more.

'But wouldn't it be better for someone like me to work closely with the family, to present the public with the truth, rather than allow the constant speculation to continue?' She forced herself to meet and hold his hard gaze. 'The various rumours that have circulated about her disappearance after her last performance haven't been all that flattering.'

There was a lengthy pause before he came from behind his desk in two easy strides and stood before her. Emily shifted in her seat, her throat threatening to close over as she had to crane her neck even further to hold his gaze.

'Just how closely are you prepared to work with my family?' he asked in a voice as smooth as velvet.

Emily swallowed. 'I...really want to do this book. I'm prepared to do whatever it takes.'

One of his brows rose speculatively. 'How very intriguing. I don't think I've met anyone quite so passionate about their work before.' His dark gaze followed the path of her nervous tongue, snaking out to moisten her dry lips. 'It makes me wonder if all that passion could have some other, more pleasurable outlet.'

Emily could feel the warmth of his body within inches of hers. She'd only have to lift one of her damp hands from under her thighs where she'd trapped them to touch him. Her stomach hollowed at the thought of those hard thighs touching hers, that strong mouth commandeering hers, those masculine hands touching her in places she secretly ached to be touched...

'I...I think it's time I left,' she croaked, getting to her feet with no trace of her usual grace and ease of movement.

On the way up her foot caught the edge of the chair-leg and pitched her forward awkwardly. He caught her easily, steadying her in the strong band of his arms, his warm, minty breath caressing her startled face.

'What's the hurry, Miss Sherwood? Or perhaps I should call you Emily, since you're so keen on getting up close and personal with my family?'

Emily tensed as she felt his hands slide down her arms to grasp both of hers in his. She felt the brush of his thighs against hers and her breathing quickened in spite of her earlier determination to maintain a cool composure in his disturbing presence.

'Let me go,' she said, wishing she didn't sound quite so breathless.

She felt his hands tighten fractionally on hers.

'But I thought you wanted to get close to us Margates?' he taunted, pulling her even closer into his body. 'Really close.'

'I've changed my mind,' she said, and tried to remove herself from his iron grasp, but his hold, though unbruising, was very firm.

'I'm disappointed. I thought you had more spirit.'

'I've got more sense than to allow you to—'

'Allow me to what? Kiss you?' His eyes caught her defiant ones. 'Or what if I were to take it one step further?'

'I'll scream,' she warned. 'And I'll report you for assault. You have no right to hold me against my will like this, and I— '

His mouth closed over her tirade and her instant response to his lips on hers betrayed her even further. Her mouth opened under the pressure of his searching tongue as his hard thighs ground against the softness of hers. His tongue explored her mouth at a leisurely pace, and although a part of her knew she should be clawing at his face to stop him her hands had somehow found their way around his neck instead, and embedded themselves into the thick pelt of his dark hair just above his collar.

He let her go abruptly and she almost fell, clutching at the edge of his desk for support.

'I can see why Danny's so taken with you,' he said, putting her from him. 'But I'm not going to fall for your undoubted charms and spill the beans quite so readily as my brother.'

'You're not close, are you?' she observed.

'You know what they say—you can choose your friends but not your relatives.'

'Yes, I do know that.'

He must have sensed something in her tone, for his penetrating gaze captured hers once more.

'Family loyalty is very important to me. I will do anything to maintain it.'

'I'm sure that's very admirable.'

'You probably have no idea how far I'd go to protect my aunt.'

'I think I'm getting the picture,' she answered. 'You've shown absolutely no scruples so far.'

He surveyed her face for a long moment.

'Is this how you usually go about interviewing people for your books? Apart from those you sleep with first?' His tone dripped with sarcasm as his dark brown eyes ran over her suggestively.

She lifted her chin defiantly, her eyes flashing.

'I assume you're referring to your brother?'

'I'm sure he won't be the only one, but, yes, I was referring to him.'

'Your brother has been a fount of information,' she lied.

Damien's mouth twisted.

'No doubt he has, given the temptation.' His eyes slid to her breasts and took their time returning to her face. Emily's spine went rigid with anger and her hands tightened into fists at her sides.

'Mr Margate—' she fought her temper back under control '—I am researching an accurate biography on your aunt's life. As I in no way wish to alienate her relatives I was hoping I could interview members of her family in order to present the public with an authentic account of both her personal and professional life. If you don't co-operate then I'll have to resort to other means.'

'Why bother coming to me? Why not do what you people usually do and make it up as you go?'

'I don't work like that,' she said. 'I believe in telling it as it is. That's why I want this to be an authentic account. Your aunt was—I mean is—a special person and—'

'My aunt is no longer public property,' he said implacably. 'You might think bedding my younger brother gives you automatic licence to document everything to do with the Margate name, but I'm afraid you're sadly mistaken.'

'When did you last see your aunt?' she asked.

'That's none of your business. Now get out.'

'But surely—'

'I said get out, Miss Sherwood, and I meant it.'

Emily drew in a deep breath, her colour high.

'Mr Margate, I don't wish to cause trouble, but I—'

'Get the hell out of here. Do you hear me?'

Emily turned and slammed the door behind her, her legs shaking in reaction. She fumed at her own cowardice all the way down in the lift. She berated herself for not standing up to him, for not calling his bluff, but somehow he'd made her feel so pathetic. She'd felt like a mangy cat scrambling for crumbs at his feet. How was she to write this book without help from Rose's nearest relatives? Rose had never married, never had children. Damien and Danny were her only living relatives since their father, her brother Donald, had died.

Emily didn't want to speculate. She didn't want to rely on innuendo or gossip. She wanted to write the truth about a woman the public had loved and still missed. She didn't want a repeat of *Tyson's Trial*. She didn't want to fail this time. She *couldn't* fail this time.

* * *

Danny called her at lunchtime. Emily had her arms full of washing and had to balance the phone against her chin to speak to him.

'I'm sorry about last night,' he said. 'How did the cocktail party go?'

'Fine.' She grimaced as her pink g-string fell to the floor. 'I won an award for *Going For Vote*. Your brother was very...'

'Damien?' Danny blurted. 'Was he there?'

Emily frowned as a hand-towel joined her g-string at her feet.

'Didn't you ask him to fill in for you?'

'The last thing my brother would do is help me,' Danny said bitterly. 'I wonder what he's up to?'

'Yes, well, that's exactly the same question I was wanting to ask you,' Emily said.

'I was going to tell you—' Danny began.

'Before or after we had sex?'

'You must think I'm an absolute cad.'

'Suffice it to say I had noticed the family likeness.'

'So, you've had dealings with Damien, then?' His tone was dry.

'You could call it that.'

'I hope he wasn't too hard on you. He can be a little protective of Rose.'

'A little protective?' Emily gave a snort of derisive laughter which sent two more articles of clothing to the floor. 'Anyone would think he was her son, the way he carries on—'

There was silence at the end of the line.

Emily stared at the pile of clean washing on the floor in front of her, their tumbled disarray not unlike the thoughts in her head.

'Danny? Is that possible? Could Damien be Rose's own son?' she asked, clutching the telephone with both hands.

'Don't be ridiculous, Emily—you know Rose never married.'

'That's not what I asked. Could Damien be her son? A child from a relationship in her past?'

'Damien's my older brother. He's four years older than me, and even though he doesn't necessarily look like me he's very much like my father.'

'But you don't get on, do you?'

'Lots of brothers don't get along. It doesn't mean they're not related.'

'But haven't you ever wondered? I mean, Damien being so different from you. You told me several times that he and your parents were often at loggerheads.'

'You told me the same thing yourself—that's just Damien. He's got a chip on his shoulder, that's all. If I were you I'd give him a wide berth. He doesn't always play by the rules and I wouldn't want to see you get hurt.'

'I'm touched by your concern for my feelings,' she said with heavy irony.

'Emily, I really am sorry about last night, but Louise and I go back a long way.'

'All the same, you could've told me yourself. It wasn't very pleasant having your brother there to gloat over my dismissal.'

'You're not dismissed. Can't we still be friends?'

'That depends a little on your brother.'

'What do you mean?'

A vision of Damien's threatening expression crowded her mind.

'Never mind. I'll talk to you later. I've got things to do.'

Emily gathered up the fallen clothes and dumped them on the nearest sofa. She went to her research file to look for the collection of Margate family photographs Danny had given her to copy. Laying them around her on the floor, she inspected each of them once more.

There were numerous ones of the infant Danny, his platinum hair standing on end as he frolicked in the shallows of the surf, or chased after a shaggy-looking dog with a ball. However, the photographs containing Damien seemed to be an afterthought. He always seemed to be to one side of the camera focus. Was it a coincidence? Or was it a deliberate attempt to shut the dark and brooding boy out of the family centre?

There was a larger photograph of the boys' father, Donald Margate, tall and austere-looking as he gazed out over the top of his shining car. Emily could see Damien's likeness in the breadth of shoulders and sooty hair. Their mother, Cora, had a flowered scarf tied around her ash-blonde hair, her pretty face wistful. As Emily searched back through each of the photographs she came to realise with an uneasy feeling that the only time Cora Margate smiled was when she was looking at her younger son, Danny. Why hadn't she seen all this before?

Emily put the photos to one side and considered her next move. She had a week before she signed the preliminary contract with her publisher. A week before Damien Margate's threats could be activated. A week to find out the truth.

Clarice phoned her half an hour later with four engagements for her in as many hours.

'You're being interviewed first thing Monday for the breakfast show,' she said gleefully. 'After that it's straight to the radio studio at NMDA. Then there's a morning tea meeting with the editor of *Writers' Review* and after that an interview with Nadine Brereton and Damien Margate.'

'*What?*' Emily gasped.

'Nadine Brereton—you know, from that current affairs programme on pay TV. She wants to—'

'I know who Nadine is,' Emily said agitatedly. 'But why Damien Margate?'

'I thought you'd be thrilled. What a coup this is! The nephew of Rose has finally agreed to an interview.'

'But I've had numerous interviews with Danny—'

'I know, my love, but he's just a boy compared to Damien Margate. He's the one with the inside information on Rose's whereabouts. He's the one you should've been setting your sights on, not that perfidious little playboy who doesn't know when to keep either his lips or his zip shut.'

Emily grimaced at the bald truth of Clarice's observation. Danny Margate *was* shallow and self-absorbed. Damien, however, was something else. She wasn't sure she could handle him. She wasn't even sure she wanted to try. What if he told the interviewer of his plans to sue? What if her editor heard the interview? How could she stop him from destroying her publicly?

'Tell me the times—I'll be there,' she said to Clarice, rummaging for a pen and paper. She jotted down the engagements and rang off, assuring her agent-cum-publicist that she'd be there with bells on, even though deep inside her courage was slipping alarmingly.

She dressed with care for the morning programme. Her hair was neatly styled into a slick French chignon and her subtle make-up was perfect. Her slim-fitting suit was hardly designer, but its shell-pink suited her colouring and, with a string of pearls and matching earrings, it would have to do. She faced the male interviewer with feigned confidence as he asked her about her research for *Rose's Cupboard*, even announcing the various outlets where she'd be present signing her other two books. But once the bright lights of the cameras moved off her face she couldn't wait to escape.

'Well done.' Clarice beamed. 'I liked the way you hesitated over the question about Damien Margate, and the delicate blush was perfect.'

'I wasn't blushing.' Emily rounded on her in irritation. 'Those damn camera lights are hot as hell.'

Clarice smiled, her eyes sparkling.

'Come on,' she said, taking Emily's arm. 'We've got to get to NMDA before nine and the traffic's horrendous.'

Emily followed in her wake, her legs starting to tremble at the thought that in less than two hours she was going to have to face Damien Margate in person.

CHAPTER FOUR

AFTER Emily finished the radio interview, which barely lasted three minutes and was in her opinion a complete waste of time, she joined Clarice in the foyer of the Regent Hotel near the Rocks. Clarice had already ordered her a lime and soda, and pushed it towards her when she sat at the table.

'Nadine telephoned to say she'll be a few minutes late. She's organised to interview you and Damien in one of the hotel suites upstairs.'

Emily felt uncomfortable at the implied intimacy of such an arrangement. A hotel suite? She and Damien Margate?

Clarice checked the diamond-studded watch on her wrist. 'He's late.'

'He's not late,' Emily said, picking up her drink. 'He's tactical.'

Clarice's eyebrows rose. 'You know him intimately, then?'

Emily shook her head. 'No, but I know how his type works. He's a power freak. It wouldn't do for him to be here early, pacing the joint, at everyone else's mercy. He'll come at the last minute as if it's him that's conducting the interview, not Nadine Brereton.'

Clarice took a deep, reflective sip of her gin and tonic.

'You really should've been a crime writer, darling. You're so good at reading people.'

'Not all people.' Emily pushed her drink to one side. 'But there's something about Damien Margate that intrigues me.'

'He is rather sexy. Tall, dark and brooding,' Clarice mused.

Emily flicked a fiery glance at her agent. 'He's a stuck-up pig. I wouldn't give him the time of day if I had a choice—'

Clarice suddenly got to her feet and extended a rose-tipped hand to someone just beyond Emily's left shoulder. 'Mr Margate! How good of you to join us.'

Emily wished the floor would open and swallow her, but seemingly the architects responsible for the plush interior of the Sydney Regent had not adequately prepared for such contingencies. The floor under her feet remained resolutely stable. However, the hand she reluctantly offered trembled as she extended it towards him.

'Mr Margate,' she said, forcing herself to meet his eyes.

'Miss Sherwood.' He nodded, his dark gaze raking her mercilessly as his hand swallowed hers.

'Nadine won't be a moment,' Clarice gushed. 'She's setting up a suite for you both.'

Damien's brows rose speculatively as he turned his gaze back to Emily. 'That sounds promising.'

Emily refused to respond to his satirical look and instead turned to inspect the menu on the table in front of her.

'I saw you on the breakfast show,' he said, taking the chair next to hers.

Emily had no choice but to look at him. 'I'm surprised. I thought you had no time for the media,' she said, re-inspecting the menu.

'I like to keep myself informed of the latest developments,' he commented drily.

Emily shrugged dismissively. 'I hope you weren't disappointed.'

'On the contrary. I was surprised you spoke so magnanimously of me.'

She met his dark gaze levelly. 'I could have said a whole lot more, but kind of figured the PG rating of the show would preclude the bit about you forcing yourself on me.'

He didn't even flinch. 'I didn't realise you had such scruples,' he said with a wry twist to his mouth. 'Perhaps I should've gone for broke.'

She glared at him, sparks of vitriol brightening her blue eyes. 'In your dreams, Mr Margate,' she drawled insolently.

He laughed as he shifted his chair to make way for the approaching Nadine, her film crew trailing her like devoted slaves.

'That remains to be seen,' he said cryptically and, standing, turned to greet the crew.

They were led to one of the deluxe suites where the lighting men were already setting up. Cameras were being positioned and make-up assistants buzzed about with palettes of foundation to counteract the harsh lighting on Nadine Brereton's face.

'Now, if Miss Sherwood would sit here—' Nadine directed her with a perfectly manicured hand '—and if Mr Margate sits here, next to me, we can get things rolling. Ready Joe?'

The head cameraman nodded as he focused in on his subjects.

'Hello, and welcome to *Afternoon Muse*. This is Nadine Brereton reporting live from the Regent Hotel, and with me are two intriguing guests. Firstly, I have beside me a biographer who is proposing to write about the illustrious, and may I say somewhat mysterious life of one of Australia's most noted stage actresses, Rose Margate. I also have with me the nephew of Ms Margate, Mr Damien Margate, who has kindly agreed to an interview. Firstly, Miss Sherwood, is it true that you are currently facing intense family opposition in order to document Ms Margate's life?'

Emily faced the camera squarely, her expression determined. One whiff, she reminded herself, and her contract would be shredded along with her career.

'No, not exactly. One family member has been incredibly

generous with his time and attention. His input has been crucial to my research.'

Damien's derisive snort was audible to Emily, but she hoped it would be edited out in the short delay to transmission.

'That would be Rose's other nephew, Danny Margate?' Nadine clarified.

Emily nodded. 'Danny Margate is extremely fond of his aunt and wanted an authentic and accurate account of her life for the public to enjoy.'

'Is it true that you haven't actually interviewed Ms Margate personally?'

'That's correct.'

Nadine Brereton tilted her head in an imitation of puzzlement. 'But how can one document someone's life accurately without having directly interviewed the person?' she asked.

'Biographies don't usually give word-for-word accounts of people's lives. Very often biographies of famous people are written long after they have passed away. Writers use various sources of information, such as journals, photographic records, interviews with close friends and family,' Emily explained.

'But the Margate family—apart from Danny Margate, that is—have been most uncooperative, isn't that correct?'

Emily glanced at Damien, who was still sitting to one side of her, his expression inscrutable.

'I'm sure they have their reasons,' she said diplomatically.

'Mr Margate.' Nadine turned to Damien. 'What is your major objection to Miss Sherwood's account of your aunt's life?'

Damien's eyes slid from Emily's to face the camera.

'I have no objection to biographies *per se*. I do, however, have an objection to biographies that are written against the express wishes of family members.'

'So you've been against this from the outset? Is that correct?' Nadine probed.

Emily's hands tightened in her lap and her breath stalled in her chest as she waited for his reply to Nadine's question.

'My aunt Rose chose to leave public life fifteen years ago. She gave more than thirty-five years of her life to her fans, oftentimes leaving little time for herself. She has not in any way authorised this account of her life and therefore neither do I.'

'Is it true that you intend to take legal action if this book, *Rose's Cupboard*, is released as planned?'

Damien's expression became shuttered. 'I am hoping to avoid legal action,' he said, flicking a glance Emily's way.

Emily crossed her fingers and prayed her editors were so busy with their huge slush pile they wouldn't be watching.

'Miss Sherwood—' the camera swung back to Emily '—are you prepared to fight for your right to write *Rose's Cupboard*, no matter what it takes?'

Emily met the dark challenging stare of Damien's eyes before turning back to Nadine.

'Months of work have gone into researching this book. Rose Margate has thousands of fans who long to hear about her life, especially since she disappeared from the theatre. This book will be a collection of photo memorabilia as well as an account of her earlier years, which I'm sure will be of great interest to many.'

'Mr Margate—' Nadine addressed Damien once more '—there will be many who no doubt agree with Miss Sherwood. What harm can it do to have a collector's item such as *Rose's Cupboard* to celebrate the magnificent achievements of one of Australia's most loved actresses?'

'If *Rose's Cupboard* was going to be written with the express wish of highlighting the many outstanding achievements of my aunt I would have no objection. However, Miss Sherwood already has a reputation for exploiting those she chooses to write about, sometimes with tragic consequences. I have nothing against Miss Sherwood trying to make a living, but I am determined she will do it with someone other than a member of my immediate family as her subject.'

Emily rose angrily in her chair, but the cameraman had swung to Nadine, who was wrapping up for a commercial break at the director's urgent signal.

'Looks like you, the public, will have to decide for yourselves. Is biographer Emily Sherwood exploiting the Margate name for her own gain? Or is she simply offering the public a treasured documentation of a much loved celebrity's life? You know the e-mail, you know the phone number, you know the channel,' she quipped. 'Let me know what your opinion is. Thank you to my guests, and when we return I'll be speaking with the head of the new emergency clinic recently opened at St Stephen's Private Hospital. Back in a moment.'

'That man is going to need more than an emergency clinic before I've finished with him!' Emily hissed at Clarice as she swept past the camera tripods.

'Now, now, my pet,' Clarice soothed. 'Think of the extra sales after that little exchange. That's exactly the sort of publicity you need.'

Emily glared across to where Damien was standing talking to Nadine Brereton. He looked back at her, his eyes darkening challengingly as they meshed with hers. She turned on her heel and swept from the room, not caring whether Clarice was ready to leave or not. She had to get out of there, and fast, before she lost control. Never had she felt so angry. Damien Margate had manipulated the interview to cast her in the role of devious money-hungry reporter, stopping at nothing to get a cheap story.

She stomped towards the nearest lift, stabbing at the call button savagely.

'Miss Sherwood?'

Emily swung round at the sound of his deep voice.

'Don't you ''Miss Sherwood'' me, you—you—bastard!'

His brows rose at her vehemence as the lift opened behind her. She stepped in and tried to block him joining her. The lift doors pinged open against the steel of his outstretched arm and she moved to the back of the carriage, her back tight against the wall, her eyes blazing with rage.

'I want to talk to you,' he said calmly.

'You just did,' she spat. 'In front of about three million people!'

'In private. No cameras, no interviewers.'

'Why?' She regarded him suspiciously. 'So you can touch me up when you feel like it?'

His jaw clenched and she felt a thin thread of victory at cracking his cool composure.

'You didn't offer too many objections at the time,' he reminded her ungallantly.

She didn't have the chance to retaliate as just then the lift doors opened and he began shepherding her out towards the hotel exit.

'What are you doing?' She tugged at his hold on her arm. 'I'm not going with you!'

Damien's hold tightened as he signalled for the concierge to hail a cab.

Emily was speechless. His hand around her slim wrist was biting into her flesh, and even though she dragged her feet as he tugged, her body kept following in his wake as if of its own volition.

He bundled her unceremoniously into a cab and barked out an address that in her distress and anger she didn't quite catch.

'This is abduction!' she railed. 'Excuse me!' She tapped on the perspex shield surrounding the cab driver. 'This man is abducting me—please take me to the nearest police station.'

The cab driver just smiled, muttered something and shook his head uncomprehendingly. Emily glared at the driver's identification photo on the dashboard and swore. The name printed there was as foreign as his heavy, unintelligible accent, and she stamped her foot in anger and frustration.

'I'll have you charged,' she flared at Damien.

'You and whose army?' he mocked.

She ground her teeth and dug her nails into his arm where it still had hold of her other wrist.

'Stop it, you little wildcat!' He swore as he sucked at his arm.

A funny sensation pooled in Emily's lower belly at his action. Her breath caught in her lungs as she watched as his mouth salved the broken skin of his forearm.

The cab pulled in to the kerb and Emily instantly recognised Damien's Double Bay house. He reached across to pay the fare and she flinched as his arm brushed against her breast.

'Get out,' he said, opening the door for her.

'Get lost.'

He reached for her wrist with an exasperated sigh and she found herself bundled out on to the pavement with little regard for either the short skirt she was wearing or the expensive silk stockings which hadn't appreciated the seatbelt buckle on the way past.

'Now look what you've done!' She indicated the long ladder running up under the hem of her skirt.

'Touché,' he said, indicating the blood-lined scratch on his arm with a sardonic tilt of his dark head.

She had no choice but to accompany him inside. He practically frogmarched her to the front door, deactivating the alarm on his way through, only letting go of her arm once the heavy door had shut behind him.

She faced him mutinously, her chest still pumping with fury at his mishandling of her. 'If you so much as lay a finger on me I swear I'll—'

'Shut up,' he said. 'I'm not going to hurt you.'

Emily crossed her arms protectively across her chest. 'Then why the kidnap routine? Or is this how you usually ask a girl round for coffee?'

He gave a disarming laugh.

Emily felt her own mouth twitching but clamped her teeth down to stop it. He had a nice laugh; she'd give him that. Deep and melodious. And the way his dark brown eyes crinkled at the corners softened his normally harsh features, making him almost handsome.

'Would you like some coffee?' he asked, still smiling.

She shook her head.

'I want to go home.'

'Well, I'm going to have a coffee, so come and talk to me while I get it ready.' He left her standing there, so, rather than stare at her own outraged reflection in the huge mirror in the foyer, she followed him into the spacious kitchen down the hall.

'If you weren't researching my aunt what would you be working on right now?' he asked conversationally, and she wished she'd stayed put. She didn't want to talk to him about herself. She didn't want to talk to him, period.

'Nothing,' she said despondently, perching on a stool against the granite bench. 'More's the pity.'

'Money troubles?' he asked, reaching for the kettle.

'Not if I get an advance on this book,' she said, giving him a hard look, wondering if he'd been investigating her financial records.

He spooned ground coffee into the jug and filled it with boiling water, then leaned back to study her.

'I hope you understand that this is nothing personal. I don't wish you to face financial ruin, but then neither do I wish to see my aunt exploited to pay for your next holiday.'

'Nothing personal?' she fired at him. 'You damn near assaulted me! What could be more personal than that?'

'As is typical of people with your choice of career, your imagination is once again working overtime.'

'And I suppose it was my imagination that ripped my stockings to shreds and dislocated my wrist?'

He closed the distance between them and picked up her

arm, turning it over in his hands as gently as if it were priceless porcelain.

'No bruises,' he said, letting it go again.

She pouted and cradled her arm against her stomach.

'It still hurt like hell.'

As he depressed the filter his gaze settled on the petulant bow of her mouth.

'You are such a drama queen. You're wasted as a writer—I can think of at least three daytime soaps you'd slot into brilliantly.'

She spun away from his mocking smile and moved to inspect the view from the kitchen window.

'How do you have your coffee?' he asked.

'Black with—' Then she remembered she wasn't having coffee. 'Nothing. I'm having nothing.'

He poured two mugs of coffee and handed her one.

'The sugar's on that shelf behind you; teaspoons are in the drawer in front of you.'

Emily breathed in the aroma of freshly ground coffee and wished she hadn't been so adamant. She'd been up since four a.m. and the breakfast show had offered her everything but breakfast.

Damien leaned his hip against the granite bench and sipped his drink, his eyes never leaving her face.

'I have decaf, if you'd prefer,' he offered laconically.

'What I'd prefer is you being straight with me. What's the point of all this?' She waved her arm to encompass the scene before them. 'You didn't bring me here to have coffee.'

'The coffee's a bonus.'

She rolled her eyes expressively. 'Let's cut through the play-acting and get to the point. What do you want from me?'

He pushed himself away from the bench and closed the distance between them. He put his coffee cup down beside her own untouched one and his eyes locked with hers. She drew in a sharp little breath that pricked at her lungs all the way down.

'I told you what I wanted the other day,' he said, his voice gravelly and deep.

Her eyes flickered to his mouth and back to his chocolate gaze.

'I...I can't do that.' She swallowed. 'I just can't.'

'Can't or won't?'

She licked her bone-dry lips, fighting for time. 'Please, I need to write this book and I need it to sell. You're in finance—surely you must know how it is? I can't survive without it. I have commitments, a mortgage—'

'Withdraw the book proposal and I'll see to your commitments.'

'What?' She gawped at him.

'You heard. Withdraw it and I'll settle all your debts.'

'You can't be serious?' She stared at him incredulously. 'Surely there must be some sort of catch?'

'There is,' he stated simply.

'And that is?'

He paused. She held her breath, somehow knowing instinctively that she wasn't going to like this. She was right.

'I want you to marry me.'

Emily's mouth dropped open and her eyes threatened to pop right out of her head. 'Is this some sort of sick joke?' she asked once her voice returned.

He lifted one shoulder in a careless shrug. 'No joke— I'm serious.'

She stared at him in horror. 'You'd go *that far* to stop me?'

He shrugged again. 'Take it or leave it. I have the means to set you up so you don't have to pen another unscrupulous word.'

'I can't believe you'd go to such lengths—'

'It would be a marriage in name only,' he said.

'Now who's auditioning for a daytime soap?' she quipped drily.

'I mean it. I find myself in the unenviable position of needing a wife on paper. Taxes and so on, if you understand.'

'I hear there are desperate women in Asia looking for an Australian passport,' she put in.

'I've decided that you'll do.'

'I'm flattered—I think.' She frowned at him darkly. 'Tell me, what was it that won you? My looks, or my way with words? Or perhaps it was that glimpse you got of my inner thigh when you slaughtered my stockings in the taxi?'

He laughed and reached for his coffee. 'I've changed my mind.' He chuckled. 'You'd be wasted on a daytime soap. You deserve your own show.'

'I'm glad you're finding this amusing because I sure as hell am not. What am I supposed to say to my agent, not to mention my publisher?'

He sipped at his coffee in a leisurely manner before answering her. 'I think you should tell them you're getting married and wish to stall the writing of your book for a few months.'

'Months?'

'Weeks, then,' he acceded. 'Who knows? By then, if you behave yourself, I might even arrange for you to interview Rose personally.'

Emily stared at him, her heart leaping in her chest. 'You'd allow that?'

He shrugged again. 'Let's wait and see. I'll make a decision after we're married.'

'So, either way you win?'

'That depends on the way you look at it,' he said smoothly. 'You stand to gain the biggest scoop of your career in exchange for being my wife.'

'I guess you're right,' she said, reaching for her nearly cold coffee. 'It depends on the way you look at it.'

CHAPTER FIVE

DAMIEN watched the play of emotions on Emily's face as she stoically finished her coffee.

'There are a few issues we need to discuss if you do decide to take me up on my offer,' he said as she put her cup down.

'What sort of issues?' She looked up at him suspiciously.

'A marriage of convenience is exactly that. One of convenience, hopefully for both parties.'

'Oh, really?' Her look was scathing. 'Do I get three guesses as to who's the winner in these particular convenience stakes?'

'I know you like to think you're paying the ultimate price, but in reality if you refuse you might be missing out on the chance of a lifetime.'

She shot him another scornful look over her shoulder as she strode towards the front door. 'You must think I'm a complete fool if you think for one minute I'd accept your offer of marriage.' She wrenched at the doorknob but before she could turn it Damien's large hand closed over hers and turned her effortlessly to face him.

'Think about it, Emily,' he said in that silky tone that sent shivers of reaction up her spine every time. 'No more money worries. No more deadlines. You could sit back and relax, just do what you want to do, write exactly what you want to write, without the pressure of others' expectations.'

'And what exactly is it you get?' she asked, trying to create some distance between the heat of their bodies.

He took his time answering. His eyes scanned her face for long seconds before dipping to the shadow between her still heaving breasts, returning to her outraged blue gaze with an unreadable light in his own.

'I get the privilege of your charming company. What more could a man want?'

Emily's resentment knew no bounds at his taunting tone. She scowled at him furiously and tried to remove her hand from his but he held her firm.

'I won't sleep with you,' she said flatly.

'So.' His mouth tilted in a sardonic grin. 'You are tempted to accept my offer?'

'Of course not!' She gave her hand a vicious tug and freed herself. He laughed and opened the door behind her. 'Come on,' he said. 'I'll take you home. We can talk about this some more in a few days.'

Emily followed him out to where he had two luxurious sports cars garaged. She set her mouth in a tight line and muttered as she got into the Lamborghini he'd opened, 'I think it's disgusting for people to have more than one car. You can only drive one at a time anyway, so what's the point other than to show off an obscene amount of wealth?'

Damien slid into his own seat and started the car with a throaty roar before glinting across at her. 'Tell me, Emily. How many pairs of shoes do you have?'

'Shoes?' She looked at him blankly.

'I'll rephrase my question. How many pairs of feet do you have?'

'One, but that's totally different and you know it. I need different shoes for different outfits. A car is a car. It gets you from A to B and that's all you need it to do.'

'I use my cars in much the same way you would use shoes. It depends on my mood.'

'So what sort of mood are you in on a Lamborghini day?' she asked, twisting slightly to look at him.

He returned her look with a dark glint in his deep brown eyes. 'You'd better put your seat belt on, Emily,' he warned. 'You're in for one hell of a ride.'

Emily sucked in her breath and snapped the belt into

place. But, although his driving was both fast and powerful, somehow she knew he wasn't talking about the car.

Emily didn't know whether to be relieved or resentful when she heard nothing from Damien Margate for over a week. It was a long few days, especially as the owner of the restaurant she worked at had informed her regretfully that he no longer needed her services. The news of her dismissal couldn't have come at a worse time. She was already a month behind on her credit card repayments, and the bank had called twice about the mortgage on her small apartment. Never had she needed an advance on a book more than now, but with the looming spectre of Damien Margate standing over her she had little chance of achieving it.

She found herself thinking about him far more than she wanted. She told herself it was because she was bored with not writing, but deep down she knew it was because there was something about him that intrigued her. On the surface he presented himself as a cool and aloof man who knew how to handle any situation. He liked to be in control and engineered it wherever possible. What she didn't understand was what he was hoping to achieve by offering her a proposal of marriage. Did he think he could stop her from writing about his family simply by insisting she become a part of it? On the contrary, her joining the Margate clan, small as it was, could only assist her in her attempt to document Rose's elusive life. She'd have access to information, private information, that would ensure the success of her book.

From her precarious position it was an attractive offer. He wasn't quite the playboy his younger brother was, but Emily was starting to see that perhaps that was a good thing. Danny had been prepared to sell all the family secrets for a few simple dates and a mention on the acknowledgements page. Damien, on the other hand, was prepared to go as far as offering to marry her to stop her from revealing anything about his family. How could two brothers be so different? What possible motivation could each of them have to act in such disparate ways?

The doorbell sounded, suddenly jolting her out of her reverie, and she opened the door to find the object of her thoughts towering over her. She stood in confusion for several awkward moments, feeling threatened and excited all at the same time. It was as if she was on the edge of a precipice: one step forward and she would fall; one step backwards and the jagged jaws of her desperate financial situation threatened to consume her.

Emily teetered on the edge. Her mouth tingled in remembrance of his determined kisses. Her legs trembled at the recall of his rock-hard frame pressing against her.

'Are you going to stand there gawping at me all day or are you going to ask me in?' Damien said.

'I....' She opened the door wider and he stepped inside. 'I was expecting someone else,' she lied, to cover her confusion.

'Danny?'

'No.'

'Have you found a replacement for him yet?' he asked.

'That's none of your business.'

'I don't know about that,' he countered. 'I'd hate to think any wife of mine had someone on the side.'

'Your confidence is misplaced. I haven't said I'm going to marry you.'

He pierced her gaze with his. 'Bankruptcy is a serious state to be in. It can have all sorts of unexpected repercussions.'

'So can marriage,' she said.

'That's true, but I'm sure you'll be adequately compensated.'

Emily hoped so. If she married him she'd eventually meet his aunt, and the chance of establishing a relationship with her would give her an ideal opportunity to document her life. Maybe Rose Margate would like and trust her enough to authenticate the biography herself, without

Damien being able to stop her. It was worth a try. Besides, he'd already assured her the marriage would be on paper only. She had nothing to lose, but everything to gain.

She took a steadying breath and, lifting her face, met the penetrating look in his eyes.

'I can't imagine why you're so keen to tie yourself to someone who detests you so much.'

'I told you before—' his eyes glinted '—I like a fight.'

'Aren't you worried I might take the money and run?'

'Try it,' he said. 'See how far you get before I catch you.'

Emily's stomach did another little flip-flop. 'So—' her tone was flippant in an effort to disguise her nerves '—do I get a diamond the size of a cantaloupe? Oh, and I don't like gold; I always wear silver.'

'I'll have a marriage contract drawn up tomorrow,' he said.

'A contract?' She looked at him in alarm.

One dark brow lifted in an arc.

'You surely didn't think I'd enter into something as serious as marriage without a prenuptial contract, did you? I'm prepared to be generous—very generous—in settling whatever debts you may have accrued, but I'm not going to sit back and watch you take me to the cleaners once it's over.'

'It makes no difference to me. But I'm wondering what exactly it is *you* get out of this arrangement.'

'I told you.' He turned slightly so she had to tilt her head to keep eye contact. 'I need a wife on paper. A dependent wife will ease my tax situation, and in the process I get some sort of control over what you write about my family.'

'I take it once I become your wife everything I write will have to be first cleared by you?'

'That's the deal.'

'It's not very attractive from where I'm standing.'

'No?'

'No. I'm not used to being scrutinised so closely.'

'Don't your editors keep a close watch on you?' he asked. 'Is that why your second book flopped?'

She hated to be reminded of her failure. It was like a sword being twisted in her gut and she hated him for bringing it up now, when she needed as much confidence as possible. She gnawed her bottom lip and tried to think of a stinging reply but her mind went blank.

He must have sensed her inner distress and changed the subject. 'My lawyer will contact you. What would you prefer—church or register office?'

She shrugged dismissively, forcibly suppressing her romantic dream of being married on a sun-drenched beach. 'I don't care.'

'I'll let you know the details in a few days. It will take me a while to organise things.'

'Take all the time you want,' she said. 'Believe me, I'm in no hurry.'

His mocking laughter annoyed her beyond endurance.

'And another thing,' she added, before he could taunt her again. 'I absolutely insist on my own room and my own bathroom. I don't like sharing.'

'I'm not all that keen on sharing either,' he said. 'And I'm not just talking about bathrooms. So if you're thinking about entertaining yourself with an array of boyfriends, forget it.'

'So I'm supposed to be celibate indefinitely?' She stared at him incredulously, incensed by his double standards. Everyone knew he was having a rip-roaring affair with a colleague's wife—Danny had told her.

'For the time being,' he answered evenly.

'And what about you?' she asked. 'Are you going to take the vow of celibacy as well? I wonder how you'll explain that to what's-her-name.'

A dark glitter came into his eyes and she took a step backwards but came up against the wall. His hands settled either side of her head and she swallowed deeply, trying not to give in to the panic that thumped in her chest.

'I'll call you,' he said, and bent his head briefly to brush his mouth against hers. She felt her lips cling to his, but before she could respond he stepped away from her and turned and left without a backward glance.

Emily ran her tongue over her lips and tasted him. She fought valiantly against the impulse to peer through the window and watch him drive away, but once she heard the roar of his car she gave in to the temptation, assuring herself it was just to check what sort of car mood he was in today. She tweaked the curtain aside just a fraction to see his hand lift in a wave from the driver's window of his black Jaguar. She hastily thrust the curtain back into place. She felt exactly as if she'd been stalked by a stealthy jungle cat, just biding its time to make a final, fatal pounce.

Emily left the lawyer's office with Damien three days later, her fingers still tingling from holding the pen to the contract that had been drawn up between them. She'd signed her name and immediately felt as if she'd signed her life away—her writing life at least. Even though she'd read the fine print as carefully as she could, the words had meant very little to her. She'd been far too conscious of Damien's lean brown hand resting on the table near hers as she bent over the contract. His long lean fingers had been splayed on the desk within touching distance of hers. She had imagined those very fingers touching her in places that would thrill her senses into fervent, panting life. The words had blurred and she'd hastily scrawled her name, hoping he couldn't see how much he affected her.

The day of the wedding arrived with a speed that did little to settle the hive of nerves that had been fluttering in Emily's stomach ever since she'd signed the prenuptial contract. She glanced at the wilting roses in her hand and wondered if they were an omen. The sticky heat of October had done its worst with her makeshift bouquet, but its biggest revenge was on her hair and her dress. The former was tumbling from its diamanté clip in haphazard tendrils, and the latter was plastered to her back in sticky patches that made her feel uncomfortable.

She wondered privately why she felt so disappointed. It wasn't as if this was a real marriage in any sense of the word. Damien had presented her with an offer too good to refuse. She still felt sick to her stomach at the thought of the bills he'd paid on her behalf, but tried to reassure herself that he'd known exactly what he was letting himself in for—as she had too.

A paper marriage. She couldn't help a wry inward smile. What the hell did that mean? Clarice had been surprisingly accommodating at the news. She thought it was all a publicity stunt and encouraged Emily to milk it for all it was worth. Emily hadn't enlightened her. She didn't want to face her agent's rage at her decision to postpone the book just yet. Besides, it suited her to keep her own motives for accepting Damien's offer under wraps. They weren't all that clear in her own head, let alone easy to explain to anyone else. She kept telling herself it was purely because of her financial situation. And because it would throw her into the pathway of Rose.

It had nothing whatsoever to do with the heat and fire of Damien's mouth on hers. Nothing whatsoever to do with the crawl of desire in her belly every time he came within touching distance. She hated him, she reminded herself relentlessly. She hated him.

And yet here she was, standing beside him before the heavily made-up marriage celebrant, who looked like an extra from a B-grade movie, repeating her vows as if she meant them, listening to the deep voice of Damien standing beside her, a silver wedding band in his hand, poised to slip on to her waiting finger.

The ring was a perfect fit and Emily wondered if that too was an omen of a different sort. Damien didn't kiss her, however. He simply thrust the ring on her finger and turned to lead her past the small gathering of his friends who'd come to witness the event.

It was ironic that Danny, not Damien, was the first to kiss her after her nuptials.

'Congratulations, Emily,' he said, hugging her far too tightly. 'I'm sure you and Damien will be very happy.'

She must have said something in reply but later couldn't recall just what it had been. She hoped it had been suitably polite and fitting for a new bride because she sure as hell didn't feel like one.

'Darling!' Clarice Connor sidled up to her, waving the mandatory champagne. 'What a clever girl! Now you're related to Rose Margate! Just think of the fame and fortune to follow.'

Emily gave a vestige of a smile. 'I'll let you know as soon as I get an interview,' she said flippantly.

It was unfortunate that Damien chose that moment to approach his new wife. Guilt at her careless words flooded her face in flushing tides as his own face clouded in suppressed anger.

'Having fun, my love?' he taunted.

'Ecstatic,' she returned. 'I can't wait for the honeymoon.'

He gave her a chilling look before he turned to speak to one of his colleagues.

The evening was interminable. Emily's fake smile made her face ache with the effort of keeping it firmly in place. She longed for a warm bath and a soothing cup of tea, but no one seemed in too much of a hurry to leave the new bride and groom to their own devices, so she had no choice but to go on pretending to be the happy, blushing bride.

Finally it was over. The last guest left and the limousine transported Damien and her back to his house in Double Bay. He opened the door and waited until she stepped through. She hesitated, her last two alcoholic drinks giving her a courage that was more foolish than Dutch.

'Aren't you going to carry me over the threshold?' she asked provocatively.

'I'm sure there's nothing wrong with your legs,' he said, brushing past her. 'Your things are in the green room,' he tossed over his shoulder as he threw his suit jacket towards the hall stand. 'Goodnight.'

Emily chewed her bottom lip. 'Goodnight,' she answered, but he'd already moved beyond the range of her soft voice.

She waited until she heard the click of his bedroom door before she moved. With dragging steps she made her way upstairs and found the room he'd allocated for her.

After a bath she curled into bed and stared sightlessly at the ceiling above her. She turned over and clamped her eyes shut on the images of her wedding day. How far from her dreams had she travelled? A mocking husband who'd married her to stop her from writing a book about his aunt. What sort of a reason for marriage was that?

Emily sat upright in bed. Perhaps her suspicions were right. Perhaps Rose wasn't his aunt at all, but more closely, intimately related. Why else would he go to the sort of trouble he had? What she hadn't been able to find out before should be much easier now she was married to Damien.

Married to Damien. The very words made her spine tingle, but she didn't know precisely which emotion precipitated it. She wasn't exactly frightened of him—not really. He made her feel agitated, angry too, but she wasn't in fear for her safety. She'd noticed on occasions how gentle he could be. Even today at the wedding he'd scooped up his friend's little girl of fifteen months and cuddled her while she undid his bow-tie with chubby fingers. He'd laughed that deep melodious laugh and Emily's stomach had shifted, wondering if...

She slammed the pillow with one fist, knocking a lamp sideways with a splintering crash. She reached blindly to retrieve it but a shard of glass pierced her hand and in the darkness she felt the stickiness of her blood dripping on to the floor.

The door flew open and a blinding light flashed on.

'What the hell happened?' Damien stood in the frame of the door, his body bare but for a pair of silky boxer shorts.

Emily's eyes squinted at the sudden light and she clutched at her bleeding hand. 'I cut myself,' she said, stemming the flow with the edge of her short nightie, which left her long legs uncovered and her bright yellow bikini briefs on show.

'How?'

'I tried to commit suicide but failed,' she said through clenched teeth.

'That's not funny,' he rasped as he stepped over the broken lamp. 'Let me look at your hand.'

She unwrapped it from the hem of her nightie and his gentle touch as he inspected the wound made her want to cry. She bit down on her lip and fought against the tears.

'It doesn't need stitching, but it needs dressing. Come to the bathroom and I'll clean it for you.'

He hesitated when she didn't move.

'Emily?' He peered at her as she huddled over her bent knees. 'Come on, it's not that serious. One bandage and you'll be as good as new.'

A tiny sob escaped and he saw the slight tremor of her slim shoulders.

'Emily?' He touched her gently on the shoulder. 'Are you OK?'

She was crying in earnest now, and he bent down to her level, one determined finger locating her wobbling chin and lifting it upwards. Her blue eyes were swimming with tears and his chest felt tight at the raw emotion reflected there.

'Perhaps we should take you to hospital,' he said. 'It might be a severed tendon or something.'

Emily pushed him away with her good hand and stumbled towards the bathroom. 'It doesn't need stitching! I'm not crying about my hand!'

'Then why are you crying?' He followed her into the *en*

suite bathroom, sidestepping the droplets of blood she left in her wake.

'I'm not crying,' she howled, reaching for the tap.

'Don't worry about the lamp.' He turned the tap on for her and handed her a face cloth. 'It wasn't anything special.'

'I'm not crying about the bloody lamp!' She sobbed into the wet facecloth, her hand stuffed into a towel like an oversized boxing glove.

Damien shook his head and gathered her into his arms, patting her slender back as she burrowed into his body.

'Is your hand hurting?' he asked.

She shook her head against his chest.

'Can I have a look at it again to make sure it's not serious?'

She nodded and unfolded herself from his arms.

He unpeeled the towel she'd wrapped around it and inspected the wound once more. The blood was slowing and he opened the cupboard above them to retrieve a bandage, which he deftly wrapped around her hand, securing the end with a tiny clip.

'There—that should keep the bleeding under control,' he said with an encouraging smile.

Emily sniffed and he reached out behind her and passed her a tissue.

'All better now?'

She nodded and mopped at her eyes.

'Sorry. Weddings always do this to me.'

His mouth twisted into an amused smile. 'Emily Sherwood—you are absolutely priceless, do you know that?'

She blinked up at him, her eyes still shiny with tears. 'Isn't my name Margate now?' And with that she burst into tears all over again.

He changed the sheets on her bed and politely left the room when she removed her blood-stained nightie to put on a fresh one. She was sitting propped up against the pillows when he returned with a glass of hot milk on a small tray.

'You look about ten years old,' he said as he set it down beside her.

'I feel about a hundred,' she replied.

He perched on the edge of her bed and handed her the glass of milk.

'Twenty-six is young to be an established author,' he observed as she sipped her drink.

'I'm not established. One bad book and it's all over.'

'Perhaps you should choose your subjects a little more carefully,' he advised.

'I intend to.'

'What will you do next? Another biography?'

She hesitated over her reply.

'I thought I might try my hand at a soap opera script. I've heard there's good money in it, and less chance of being sued.'

'Is that why you agreed to marry me?' he asked. 'Just to avoid being sued?'

She found his question unsettling. It still wasn't clear in her mind why she'd agreed to marry him.

'Getting a divorce is the same as being sued,' she said. 'Lots of money changes hands and everyone ends up bitter.'

He took the empty glass from her and set it back on the tray.

'You sound very cynical. Did your parents go through an acrimonious divorce?'

'Is there any other type of divorce?'

He shrugged. 'Perhaps you're right.' He got to his feet. 'Let's hope if we end this marriage we do so with respect and dignity.'

'What's with the "if"?' she asked. 'Don't you mean "when"?'

He gave her a long look before he picked up the tray

from beside her. 'This marriage will end if and when I decide.'

'Don't I have any say in it at all?'

'That depends.'

'On what?'

'I'll let you know.'

'What sort of answer is that?' She sat upright in the bed, wincing as her injured hand caught the edge of the lamp table.

'It's all the answer you're going to get for now, so be a good girl and go to sleep.'

'Stop treating me like a little kid!' she stormed. 'I'm not your daughter, for God's sake, I'm your wife.'

He put the tray back down and approached the bed, a glint lurking in the melted chocolate depths of his eyes. Emily's own eyes widened in alarm as his tall figure loomed over her prostrate form. His hands came down either side of her, effectively trapping her.

'Is that an element of pique I hear in your voice, my love?' he asked silkily.

'I'm...I'm not your love,' she said hoarsely.

'No,' he agreed, and her heart squeezed painfully in her chest. 'But you are my wife, as you so cleverly reminded me.'

'I'm...I'm not really your wife,' she croaked. 'I'm just a paper wife—remember?'

His eyes ran over her face, dipped to the shadowed cleft of her nightgown where her breasts lay secretly aching for his touch.

'You're a very beautiful and very tempting paper wife,' he said against the corner of her trembling mouth.

'Please...' She shrank back against the pillows, suddenly terrified she'd betray herself if his mouth so much as touched hers.

'Aren't paper wives allowed to kiss their husbands goodnight?' he asked, running an idle fingertip along the fullness of her bottom lip.

'I...' She ached to take his finger into her mouth. Her lips swelled with the need to feel his tongue graze hers and thrust into the moist cavern of her mouth. Her legs sagged against the mattress with the weight of need as he leaned inexorably closer.

'Goodnight, Emily,' he said, planting a soft breath-like kiss on her mouth. Then he lifted himself away from her and, picking up the tray, closed the bedroom door behind him on his way out.

CHAPTER SIX

IT WAS a long night. Emily tossed and turned, trying to find a comfortable spot for her hand and a restful space for her tortured mind, but both eluded her. She watched as the sun rose defiantly in the east as if to spite her, its searing heat an added insult to her sleep-deprived state of mind.

Damien was in the kitchen when she came downstairs, looking disgustingly refreshed and handsome in a dark business suit and light blue shirt with perfectly toned tie.

'Good morning. Did you sleep well?'

'No, I did not,' she snapped irritably.

His gaze slid to her bandaged hand. 'Hand giving you trouble?'

'A bit.'

'Are you a breakfast girl?' he asked, reaching across to pour some skimmed milk into a jug.

'A what?'

'Do you eat breakfast? Or are you one of those people who insist on skimping on the most important meal of the day?'

Emily eyed the bowl of home-made muesli he had in front of him.

'I'll have what you're having,' she said, dragging out a stool.

He handed her a bowl and the container of muesli. She went to open it but it proved too awkward for her injured hand. He got up from where he was reading the morning paper and took the container from her.

'Here, let me.' He dished out a hearty portion, then reached for the milk and began pouring. 'Tell me when.'

'When,' she said, and thanked him as he pushed the bowl and a spoon towards her.

'We made the social pages.' He pointed to the newspaper in front of him.

Emily wasn't sure she really wanted to see what the press had made of their unexpected union, but she came round and leaned over his shoulder all the same.

'I look fat.'

He chuckled in amusement. 'You look beautiful.'

She sat back down opposite and toyed with her cereal, her brow furrowing as she relentlessly chased a sultana around her bowl.

'What's the matter?' he asked. 'Not regretting it already, are you?'

'What?' She looked across at him. 'Oh, no. I was just thinking.'

'About what?'

She crushed the hapless sultana with the edge of her spoon before looking back at him. 'Why didn't your aunt Rose come to your wedding?'

His eyes hardened as he surveyed her face. 'I was wondering how long it would take you.'

'What do you mean?' Her stomach tightened at the caustic tone of his voice.

'Here was I, thinking you'd at least wait a few days, maybe even a week or two before you made your move.'

'What are you talking about? What move?' She looked at him blankly.

He got to his feet, pushing his bowl away with an angry movement of one hand.

'It's why you agreed to marry me, isn't it? The real reason, I mean.'

She swallowed the lump in her throat and stared at him speechlessly.

'An interview with Rose was the icing on the wedding cake, isn't that right?'

'I—'

'Don't bother to deny it—it's written all over your face. Anyway, I heard you talking to your agent about it.'

'But I didn't mean it! I was joking!' She found her voice at last.

'I told you before that Rose is off limits. It will be her decision if she wants to be interviewed by anyone, and that includes you. Being married to me doesn't automatically give you any special privileges.'

'You can say that again,' she muttered darkly.

'What was that?' He snagged her uninjured arm and turned her towards him. 'You're not happy with our current arrangement? If so, I can always reinstate your mortgage and credit card debt, not to mention starting legal proceedings against anything you might be thinking of writing.'

A cold despair settled in her chest at the hatred in his eyes.

'I hate you,' she said bitterly.

'Hate is good. I can handle hate. Hate me all you like— see if I care.'

Emily pulled at his hold, desperate to escape before her anger turned to grief. 'Let me go! You're hurting me.'

'Don't push your luck with me, Emily,' he warned. 'I'm prepared to be reasonable. Don't make me regret my decision to help you.'

'Help me?' she flared at him. 'Have I missed something here?' Her lip curled in scorn. 'Oh, I get it now! You married me to *help* me. I'm so glad I've finally figured it out.'

'Sarcasm doesn't suit you.'

'Neither does marriage,' she threw at him.

'Well, I can assure you neither will bankruptcy, so let's give this a try first.'

'I'd rather starve than spend another day with you!' she retorted.

'You're acting like a child, Emily,' he reprimanded her sternly. 'Do yourself and me a favour and grow up.'

It was all too much for her. Her lack of sleep, the emotional roller coaster of her disappointing wedding day and her injured hand finally cracked her fragile hold on her emotions. She bent her head and burst into tears.

'Oh, Emily,' he groaned, and gathered her to him. 'I'm being a brute to you. I'm sorry. Hey, come on—no more tears. I prefer it when you're throwing punches at me.'

She cried all the harder and he pulled her even closer. He bent his head to the fragrant cloud of her hair and let her cry. Her soft little body was nestled against his as if it had been fashioned just for that purpose. Her breasts were jammed up against his chest and he could feel the buds of her nipples pressing through the silk of his shirt. His trousers tightened over his groin and his breathing quickened as he fought against the rising desire pumping through his veins.

'I'm sorry.' Emily came up for air, her nose bright pink and her eyes still trickling tears. 'I'm not good without sleep.'

'I'm the one who should apologise. Let's call a truce. Down all arms and see if we can get through the rest of today without a cross word.'

Emily nodded, scrubbing at her eyes with her sleeve.

'Here.' He handed her his handkerchief and she dabbed at her eyes.

'I feel foolish.' She gave the handkerchief back. 'I hardly ever cry.'

'Sorry to have that effect on you.' His tone was wry.

She looked up into his eyes and suddenly realised his arms were still around her. She could feel the muscles in his thighs pressing against hers, and the unmistakable pressure of his maleness issuing its own insistent message.

'Emily.' His body shifted slightly against hers, his eyes darkening with desire. 'This is not such a good idea.'

'What isn't?' Was that her voice? That tiny breathless whisper?

His body collided intimately again with hers and she gasped.

'Oh, *that*,' she croaked.

'Yes, that.'

There was an infinitesimal pause. She gazed up at him, her breath stalling in her throat as his eyes burned into hers. Then, as if in slow motion, his head came down towards hers. His lips moved over hers with a deepening pressure until his tongue probed and swiftly entered her mouth. Emily sagged against him, her legs weakening as his tongue danced with hers, drawing from her a response she hadn't known she was capable of.

His lips moved to the silky texture of her neck, the underside of her ear and back again to her mouth. Emily strained to get closer to him, her feminine softness moulding itself to every hard plane of his body until he groaned against her mouth, 'This is crazy.'

She didn't respond in words. Instead, she unbuttoned his shirt and released his tie with fingers not quite steady. His chest was smooth and muscled, a fine sheen of sweat already beading at the fervent touch of her searching fingers.

His hands began a search path of their own, slipping underneath her T-shirt and deftly unhooking her bra. His warm hands captured the weight of her breasts and she gasped at the sensation of his exploring fingers discovering her contours, and then his mouth, when he bent his head to their hardened peaks.

He swept back to her mouth as her hands went to his belt. He jolted at her touch, but she continued her mission with a wantonness that surprised herself even more than it did him.

She felt him press her back against the table, the urgency in his hands and tongue preparing her for the inevitable. There was no turning back. Her track pants were at her ankles, his suit trousers at his knees, his fingers searching for her slick moistness.

'Yes, oh, yes!' She rocked against his hand and he pulled her down the table until his fingers were replaced with his own heat and length. She cried out at the force of his first thrust, her legs wrapping around him tightly to prolong the sensation. He steadied himself, slowing just a fraction, his breathing ragged.

Emily gloried in the loss of control she'd evoked in him. She'd brought him to the brink of unbearable desire and even now he was struggling to keep himself in check in order to bring about her pleasure before giving in to his own.

She could see it in the passion-contorted features of his face as he drove into her. She could feel the rigid control wavering as he hunted for her mouth once more. She felt the desperation in his fingers as they located the tiny swollen nub of her desire and coaxed her towards ecstasy at the same time as his throbbing length filled her again and again as he retreated and returned, each time firmer, deeper.

She almost screamed with the pleasure of her release. She bit down on his shoulder to dampen the sound, her nails raking his back as he continued his assault on her senses. His own climax soon followed, his agonised groan of pleasure like music to her ears. She held him to her, wanting to prolong the sensation of being filled by his liquid warmth, but he was already moving from her.

'That should never have happened.' He pulled up his trousers, his eyes not quite meeting hers.

'Wasn't it good for you?' she asked pertly, adopting a pose of streetwise promiscuity when nothing could have been further from the truth. She hitched up her track pants and combed her fingers through her ravished hair as if she'd just returned from a jog around the block.

Damien gave her a sweeping glance, his eyes still reluctant to mesh with hers. 'I've certainly no need to ask you the same question,' he said. 'My back feels as if I've been on a rack, not to mention that gnaw you gave my shoulder.'

'Well, you know the saying.' She reached for the cereal bowl she had discarded earlier and picked up her spoon. 'If you can't stand the heat—get out of the kitchen.'

Damien frowned at her as he tucked in his shirt.

'Have a good day at the office,' she added, and opened her mouth over her spoon.

He picked up his tie off the floor, where she'd tossed it earlier, and draped it loosely around his neck. This wasn't how he'd planned things. Emily was up to something, he was sure. Somehow she'd switched the tables on him—quite literally, he thought, with a wry glance towards the table they'd just christened.

'I'll call you later.' He scooped up his jacket and made his way to the bathroom.

She heard him leave the house a few minutes later. The sound of his car roaring out of the driveway triggered a deep sigh in her chest as she contemplated spending the rest of the day alone.

Emily used the morning to explore Damien's house, her ears constantly pricked in case he was to return unannounced. She moved from room to room and from floor to floor to familiarise herself with her new surroundings, each room offering a clue to the mysterious man she'd married. It was a beautiful house, but it was definitely not a home. It didn't even feel particularly lived-in. Some of the rooms were stale from being unused for so long, so she opened window after window as she went through each room, stopping to rearrange the stiff cushions on the velvet sofas in the formal lounge to make them a little more welcoming.

Damien's bedroom she left well alone. As she skirted past a pool of heat trickled into her belly at the remembrance of their passionate union this morning.

Her previous experience of sex had been somewhat limited. Her first had been little more than a teenage fumble that had been embarrassingly interrupted by the boy's parents returning home. The second had been Raife Norton-Floyd, who'd claimed to love her but had already been married. The irony of her situation made her smile ruefully. Damien claimed he didn't care for her at all, and yet had married her within days of asking her. Who could make sense of men?

The garden was an outside version of the interior of the house. It, too, was beautiful in its way, but unwelcoming with its array of neatly landscaped plants that offered a green screen from the nearest neighbours but very little in the way of blossom and fragrance.

Emily sat on the sun-lounger near the pool and dangled her toes in the cool water, watching as the ripples travelled outwards in ever-widening circles. Just like her life, she reflected. The circles of her life were moving further and further beyond her control, at least ever since Damien had entered her life so forcefully.

She was a married woman, in every sense of the word. She was finally free from her crippling financial burden but shackles of a different kind had settled about her, holding her in Damien's controlling hands.

She found it difficult to unravel her feelings about him. Sometimes she thought she hated him; other times she found herself thinking about him, his darkly handsome features filling her head until there was no room for her own thoughts. She pictured his smiling mouth when she flew back at him with some witticism, and she could recall the warmth and comfort of his arms around her when she'd hurt her hand and he'd gathered her close. She didn't understand him, couldn't imagine why he'd acted the way he had in marrying her. But then she thought about the very deep and loyal love he obviously felt for Rose, stopping at nothing to protect her. If only someone, some day, would love her like that!

Emily went back into the house and fetched her purse and the set of keys Damien had given her. She walked towards the cafés and shops, stopping to buy huge bunches of flowers as well as the latest bestseller—unfortunately not her own. She grimaced ruefully as she handed over the money.

Some time later she stepped back and inspected her floral handiwork. 'Mmm, that's much better.'

She had planted spilling blossoms in each of the formal rooms, their sweet fragrance soon wafting through the long corridors.

She selected a classical choral collection CD from the state-of-the-art hi-fi console and, turning up the volume, listened as the ethereal sound filled the empty house with beatific strains that sounded as if they were coming down from heaven. She shut her eyes and wrapped her arms around herself, standing in the centre of the huge sitting room to let the magic of the perfect blend of young male voices seep into her very bones.

She didn't hear Damien's car return. Nor did she hear him enter the house. It was only when he entered the room that she sensed his presence. She swung around, her eyes springing open, her cheeks flaming.

'I...I was just listening to some music,' she gabbled in embarrassment.

'You and most of the neighbourhood, it seems,' he observed drily as he turned the volume down several notches with the remote control.

'I like it loud,' she defended.

'You can turn it up later, when you start yelling at me. But for now I want to talk to you.'

'I don't yell.'

'Don't speak too soon. We've only been married twenty-four hours.'

Emily turned away to pick up another CD, effectively dismissing him.

'Emily, look at me.'

She rolled her eyes and faced him. 'Yes?'

'I can sense you don't wish to discuss what happened between us this morning, but discuss it we must.'

'What's to discuss? It was just sex.'

'Such jaded cynicism in one so young astounds me.

Nevertheless, even people who have "just sex" must take full responsibility for having done so.'

'And your point is?' She arched one brow pertly, her pose insolent.

'Are you on the Pill?'

She couldn't hold his gaze, and instead turned to retrieve one of the fallen petals from the flowers she'd arranged on the walnut sideboard.

'Of course I'm on the Pill,' she snapped. 'And I haven't got any nasty diseases so you can breathe easy.'

'I'm glad to hear it. However, this isn't just about you—it's about me. It was wrong of me not to protect you this morning. I was a little unprepared.'

She did glance up at him at that.

'Shall I distribute condoms in each of the rooms just in case it happens again?' she asked.

'It won't happen again,' he stated implacably. 'It must *not* happen again. Is that clear?'

'So it's all my fault now? How typically male! Just because you can't control your own lust you conveniently throw it all back on me.'

'You were extremely provocative—'

'I was wearing a fluffy tracksuit, for God's sake!' Her voice rose in anger.

'You'd look sexy in a garbage bag!' he shouted.

'You'd better turn the music back on,' she threw back. 'You're shouting.'

'I'm not—' He ground his teeth and lowered his voice. 'You are so damned annoying you'd make a mute person shout. I came home early to apologise—'

'You came home to get yourself off the hook,' she fired back. 'Don't worry—there'll be no paternity suit from me. I wouldn't dream of being so irresponsible as to contribute to the replication of your likeness.'

'As I said on a previous occasion—you have a charming way with words.'

'Yeah? Well, so do you.' She turned away and plucked at the petals in her hand.

'What are all the flowers for?' he asked suddenly, noticing what she was doing. 'Who died?'

'This place is like a mausoleum. I thought it needed a little softening.'

'You're probably right. I don't spend much time at home. I hadn't noticed.'

There was a lengthy silence. Emily scrunched the petals to a mush in her hand and waited for him to continue the conversation.

'I thought we could go out for a meal this evening,' he said at last.

'I'm not hungry.'

'Come now, Emily,' he chided. 'Humour me. I hate eating out alone and there's a great Thai restaurant a few blocks from here.'

She felt herself wavering. What harm could it do to spend an evening with him? It wasn't as if she had anything to lose. In fact, she stood to gain. What if he unknowingly revealed some information about Rose? What if she were actually to find out where she was living?

She joined him downstairs twenty minutes later, dressed in a black close-fitting top and silvery-grey slim-fitting trousers that clung lovingly to her toned thighs only to swing away at her ankles in shimmering folds. She'd left her honey-brown hair to fall about her shoulders, its soft curls framing her face.

'I'm all out of garbage bags,' she quipped as his eyes ran over her.

He chuckled. 'Come on, you minx. I must have had rocks in my head to get mixed up with you.'

She didn't respond. She was still trying to figure out her own motivations for tying herself to him. She was living in his house and bearing his name while the research notes of her book lay untouched. None of it made sense. Least of all her own treacherous heart.

CHAPTER SEVEN

THE restaurant was busy but the head waiter quickly bustled across to escort them to a quiet table in the corner. Once they were seated with a chilled glass of Chardonnay in front of them Emily started to feel her shoulders relax a little. She sipped at her wine and examined the menu, all the while conscious of the strongly muscled legs occasionally touching hers under the narrow table.

'What do you fancy?'

Emily blinked up at him, her eyes wide.

'Do you like it hot or—'

'Oh!' She coloured delicately, a vision of their passionately joined bodies flashing through her brain. 'I thought you were talking about something else. Sorry—yes, I don't mind—anything will do.'

'Are you as easy-going with your choice of men as you are with your food?' he asked.

'Apparently,' she said, taking another hefty sip of her wine.

He waited until the waiter had taken their order before he spoke. 'You have a very sharp wit, Emily, but eventually it will cause you a great deal of trouble.'

'I didn't realise you were into prophecy,' she retorted. 'I thought finance was your thing.'

'How many men have you had?' His question was abruptly delivered. She picked up her glass and eyeballed him questioningly over the rim.

'Slept with. Had sex with,' he clarified at her quirked brow.

She pretended to be making some sort of mental tally as

she twirled the glass in her hands. Then, after a pause, she shook her head.

'Sorry, can't quite remember. Never was all that good at maths. How about you? You'd have a well-tallied record, being in finance and all. How many women have you had?'

His mouth twisted into a reluctant smile. 'Point taken. I'd momentarily forgotten about the Women's Movement.'

She smiled back, suddenly enjoying this light-hearted banter. 'I was worried there for a time that maybe I'd married a dinosaur.'

'Why did you marry me, Emily?'

The question came from nowhere and startled her.

'I...it seemed like a good idea at the time,' she prevaricated.

'For me, certainly,' he acceded. 'I stopped you writing your book in exchange for taking on your financial commitments. But what is it you get?'

She met his dark gaze levelly. 'I get to be wined and dined and ravished on the kitchen table,' she said flippantly, reaching again for her wine. 'What more could a woman ask for?'

His brows met together in a frown. 'Somehow I think you hide behind that mercurial wit for reasons I'm yet to discover.'

'Prophecy, finance and psychology,' she mused mockingly. 'Mmm, you are a multi-skilled man.'

'Tell me about your family.' He swiftly changed the subject.

Her eyes skittered away from his. 'I told you before, my parents died years ago.'

'You also mentioned having two siblings.'

'Did I?' She marvelled at his keen memory but refused to be drawn any further. Discussions about her family were definitely off limits.

'Brothers or sisters?' he asked.

'What is this?' She frowned at him. 'A career change for

you? Are you thinking of writing a biography on my family?'

'You seem very defensive about a few simple questions,' he observed.

'That's rich, coming from you,' she shot back. 'I can give you addresses and phone numbers, if you like. That's more than you've given me.'

'So, we're back to that again, are we?' His eyes narrowed as he looked across the table at her. 'Still hankering after the elusive interview with Rose. Was that what this morning was about? Part of the buttering-up process?'

She considered slinging the contents of her wine glass in his face, but then realised it was already empty. His gaze followed her hand as it moved towards the full tumbler of water between them.

'I wouldn't if I were you,' he warned, sliding his hand over hers. 'Not unless you never want to eat in this restaurant again.'

Just then the waiter made a timely appearance with their food and Emily had to force her anger under some sort of control. She silently fumed, poking at the grains of rice on her plate, her appetite gone.

'Try the green curry.' Damien passed her the serving dish garnished with kaffir lime leaves. 'It's reputed to be the best in town.'

He spooned some on to her plate, the fragrant aroma teasing her nostrils. She prodded her fork at the succulent pieces of chicken in the creamy coconut sauce but didn't carry any of it to her mouth.

'Stop sulking,' he said, after watching her toy with the food for endless minutes. 'Personally, I don't care if you eat it or not, but I resent having my own appetite spoilt by your petulance.'

'I'm not sulking—I'm upset. When I'm upset I can't eat.'

He gave an exasperated sigh and put down his fork. 'Emily, I didn't mean to upset you. I was just trying to make conversation with you. I wouldn't have thought it was so unreasonable for a husband to know about his wife's family.'

'Ditto.'

He gave her a hard look and she returned it with a sharp glance of her own.

'I don't wish to discuss my family. It's no one's business but my own.'

He picked up his glass and said derisively, 'Quite frankly, the only reason I'm the slightest bit interested in your family background is to find out how the hell you got so screwed up.'

Emily got to her feet and, with utter disregard for the swivelling heads of the rest of the diners, stormed from the table without a backward glance.

He caught her before she even got to the street corner.

'OK,' he conceded, taking her arm, 'that was a raw nerve. I won't touch it in future.'

She tried to shake off his hold but his other arm came around her as well.

'If you don't let me go I'll scream.' She opened her mouth in readiness but before the sound could escape his lips closed over hers. She gave a token struggle, but his mouth was determined and his arms strong as they pulled her into the warm shield of his body. She tasted wine on his tongue as it stroked along hers, drawing it into active response against his.

Somehow it didn't matter any more who was kissing whom. Damien's mouth had overpowered hers to begin with, but now her lips were conducting their own assault. She nipped gently at his full bottom lip, tugging at it with her small white teeth. He gave her an answering nip and she slid her tongue into his mouth.

He pushed her back against a high garden wall out of the glow of the street light. His lower body ground against hers as his hands found her breasts through the silk of her top.

Suddenly he stopped. His breathing was as ragged as

hers as he stepped away from her, raking a hand through his dark hair. She opened her mouth to say something, anything, but he shook his head warningly and pressed a none too gentle finger to her lips.

'Don't.'

'Buffft,' her lips protested against the pad of his finger.

He snagged her arm and began striding off towards his car, almost dragging her in his wake. Once in the car he drove silently but furiously towards home, his white-knuckled grip on the steering wheel cautioning her to remain silent.

She waited until they were back inside the house before she spoke. 'Has the embargo on my speech been lifted, or am I to—?'

'You do it deliberately, don't you?' His expression was thunderous as he loomed over her.

'Do...do what?'

His jaw clenched in anger as he fought to keep control. 'This act of beguiling charm you're so good at. One minute the injured innocent, next the seductive siren.'

'I've got no idea what you're talking about.'

He gave a scornful grunt. 'I can see what you're up to, and I've got to admit I'm tempted to throw caution to the winds and take what's on offer. But that would be playing right into your hands, now, wouldn't it?'

Emily looked at him in bewilderment. 'I think maybe I've missed something important. Can you back up a bit to that part about me looking sexy in a garbage bag?'

'There!' He threw a hand in the air expressively. 'You're doing it now.'

'What am I doing?' she asked, her eyes widening innocently.

'Never mind.' He turned away, thrusting his hands into his trouser pockets. 'I'm going away for a few days. On business.'

'When will you be back?'

'I'm not sure,' he said. 'Two, maybe three days.'

'You don't have firm plans? I thought business people like you would run to very tight schedules.'

'You're starting to sound like a suspicious wife.'

She met his satirical gaze with a disdainful flash of her blue eyes.

'I don't care what mischief you get up to while you're away. I'll be too busy planning my own.'

His eyes narrowed dangerously. 'Careful, Emily,' he warned. 'Don't forget the terms of our deal.'

'Could you run them past me one more time?' She blinked up at him guilelessly. 'I'm a little hazy on the details.'

'Don't play games with me, little lady. You know the terms. If you step out of line by speaking to the press or pursuing this notion of tracking down my aunt behind my back, watch out. The legal system will come down on you so hard you won't know what hit you.'

Emily lifted her chin defiantly. 'And what will your lawyers say when I tell them you broke your part of the deal by having sex with me? Isn't this supposed to be a paper marriage?'

He gave a contemptuous sneer. 'I'd like to see you prove it. It'll be your word against mine and I know who they'll believe.'

'You don't have such a squeaky-clean image yourself,' she retorted. 'How is Mrs Janssen, by the way?'

His expression darkened with suppressed anger. 'Be very careful, Emily. Careless words can come back to bite you.'

'Are you in love with her?' Emily asked baldly. 'Or is it just good old lusty sex?'

'I refuse to answer that.'

'Why?'

'Because it's none of your business.'

'Oh, well.' She shrugged dismissively. 'I don't care either way as long as you don't paw me instead when she's not available.'

'That's a despicable thing to say,' he ground out.

She gave a cynical little laugh. 'At least you'll be telling her the truth when you say your wife doesn't understand you. That usually reels them in, doesn't it?'

'I wouldn't know—you tell me. You're the one with the track record with married men. What did Raife Norton-Floyd do to lure you? Or were you his just for the asking?'

'I don't wish to partake in this conversation.' She swung away, her colour high.

'That's a little inconsistent of you, isn't it, Emily? You've taken pot shots at me all evening, but you don't like it when the tables are turned, do you?'

She turned back to glare at him. 'There would be absolutely no point in me discussing any of this with you because you've already made up your mind about me, and nothing I could say or do will change it.'

'Go on, try me,' he challenged her. 'Tell me you didn't have a rip-roaring affair with Norton-Floyd to get inside information on that funding scheme he was involved in. And tell me you didn't chase after my brother to filch photos and journals you had no business seeing.'

Emily couldn't think of a word to say in her own defence. She'd been caught off-guard with Raife. He'd been so polished and she so innocent she hadn't seen the potential for the disaster that eventually occurred. With Danny, she'd been lonely and he'd been friendly. She'd used him, but then, hadn't he used her as well?

'Your silence condemns you,' Damien said.

Emily turned her back on him on her way to the door, her lips clamped tight against the anger that threatened to spew out of her mouth.

'What?' he taunted her. 'No stinging parting shot?'

She paused, her hand frozen on the doorknob as she mentally counted to ten.

'I have nothing I wish to say to you,' she bit out.

'Not even goodnight?'

She swung back to face him. 'No, not even goodnight. I

hope you have a bad night—a rotten night. I hope you toss and turn and your pillow feels like lead and—'

He laughed out loud. Emily's tenuous hold on her temper snapped and she stomped back across the room to push a finger against his chest, her eyes sparking with venom.

'Don't you laugh at me!'

Damien captured her hand and she pulled against his hold, her nails embedding themselves into his palm.

'Oh, no, you don't.' He undid the clench of her fingers and, grasping both hands in one of his large ones, held them over her head.

Emily felt the wall at her back and the press of his strongly muscled thighs on hers. Her chest heaved with impotent rage against his, her breasts rising and falling against him.

'Let me go, you bastard!'

'I just love it when you talk dirty,' he drawled.

'You won't when I talk dirty to the press,' she threatened recklessly. 'When I tell them all about your affair with Mrs Janssen and about the way you forced me to marry you to cover it up.'

His brow furrowed, his hand still holding hers above her head. 'Is that what you think?'

'Isn't it true?' She glared at him frostily.

He shrugged one shoulder. 'I thought I'd made my reasons for marrying you quite clear. I wanted to stop your book being written.'

She flicked her eyes upwards to her hands in his hold. 'You wanted control of me, not just the book.'

The corner of his mouth lifted in a half-smile. 'Now, that's what I would call an impossible task. You don't even have control of yourself, let alone anyone else being able to manage it.'

'That's because you make me lose control!' she said crossly.

'Is that so?' His brow lifted speculatively as his eyes ran over her breasts, still rising and falling against his chest.

'I don't mean that way.' Her tone was scathing.

'Don't you?'

'Of course not!'

'Then what was all that about in the kitchen this morning?'

'That...that was...an accident.'

'An accident?' His lip curled expressively.

'It was your fault,' she accused. 'You started it.'

'And you could've finished it at any time, but you didn't. I wonder why, Emily?' he mused. 'I wonder why?'

'You've got tickets on yourself if you think it was anything other than the most basic animal attraction,' she spat back.

'So you do admit to feeling some sort of attraction towards me?' His brown eyes questioned hers.

'No.'

He gave a rumble of cynical laughter. 'No, of course you wouldn't. But we both know the truth, don't we?'

'The truth is I loathe and despise you.'

'But you were prepared to marry me.'

'Suffice it to say it was an offer too good to refuse.' Sarcasm coloured her tone. 'I would've settled for the Elephant Man if he'd offered to pay off my Visa card. You got there first.'

'So I did.' His eyes followed the nervous movement of hers. 'So now you're in my debt, so to speak.'

'I...' She moistened her dry lips. 'I don't quite see it that way.'

Damien's hands slid down from around her up-raised wrists and instead settled on her waist. Emily stiffened. Her hands had nowhere to go but his shoulders, where they valiantly tried to push him away. But somehow the feel of his firm muscles under her palms distracted her from her task of putting as much distance between them as possible. His shirt was silky to the touch, his shoulders warm and broad underneath the pads of her fingers.

His eyes sought and held hers. She felt like a moth attracted to a searing flame in spite of the danger it represented, and the one thing she was becoming more and more certain of was that Damien Margate spelt danger.

'Be a good girl while I'm away, Emily,' he said, his fingers now light, almost like a caress about her waist.

She didn't trust herself to answer. Her breath had stalled somewhere in the back of her throat at his nearness, his touch feather-light but electric all the same. All her nerves seemed to be leaping inside her body, each portion of her flesh craving for the brush of his long fingers.

His head lowered to hers, his mouth just a fraction from hers. 'Kiss me goodbye,' he commanded her gently.

She wanted to resist. Every rational part of her being insisted she resist the temptation to press her soft lips along the firm line of his, but it was overruled by a deep and irresistible desire to feel his mouth on hers once more.

She lifted her head just a fraction and their lips touched. It was like a match to tinder; heat coursed and exploded on impact, flames of passion licking between them uncontrollably. His tongue found hers and played with it, danced with it, teased it. The answering moves of her own tongue tightened his hands about her waist, pressing her into the rock-hard wall of his chest while his lower body told her of his aching, throbbing need.

Suddenly she was free. He stepped away from her so abruptly it took her a couple of seconds to collect herself. She straightened her clothes and forced herself to make eye contact.

'Goodnight, Emily,' he said, his mouth set in a grim line.

Emily rolled her still tingling lips together before answering quietly, 'Goodnight.'

He turned and left her standing there, listening to the mantel clock ticking away the minutes like the drone of a metronome keeping time to a tedious piece of music. Emily sighed and, crossing her arms against her chest, turned and stared sightlessly out of the window overlooking the bay while the persistent clock kept time in the background.

CHAPTER EIGHT

EMILY didn't hear him leave the next morning. She'd lain awake most of the night, tossing and turning and thumping her lead-like pillow, trying to eradicate the memory of his kiss. By the time she did eventually fall into some sort of restless slumber Damien had left to catch the first flight of the day.

Later, as she made herself a small breakfast of toast and tea, she wondered if it was really consistent of her to feel lonely at the thought of him not returning to the house that night. She should be feeling relieved, she remonstrated with herself. He wouldn't be missing her! He would have no doubt arranged to meet up with his lady-love interstate, away from the prying eyes of the local press, while she, his legal wife, sat twiddling her thumbs, wondering what to do with the rest of the day.

Emily pushed her second slice of toast away; she knew she had to do something with her time or she'd end up going crazy. As it was she spent most of her time thinking about Damien, and that was surely a pathway to disaster. He wasn't interested in her other than as an entertaining diversion when his mistress was unavailable. And she didn't like him—but there was something about him that drew her to him like a bee towards scented blossoms.

Animal attraction, she'd explained to him earlier, trying to find some sort of valid excuse for her own wanton behaviour. She knew she should be feeling shame about their passionate encounter, but for some reason she didn't. She felt proud. Proud that a full-blooded man of such iron control as Damien Margate had let caution fly to the winds and let himself sink into the pleasure her young and eager body had offered.

It had been an awakening for her in more ways than one. She'd never felt such need before. She'd never felt her responses in such a wild and abandoned way, and never had she felt so complete, as if two halves of a whole had joined and the universe had sighed in relief at their union.

She wanted it to happen again but knew it couldn't. He didn't want a physical relationship with her because his only reason for marrying her was to protect his aunt. Their marriage was a sham, a façade they were both using for different reasons. The only trouble was, Emily wasn't sure what her reasons were any more.

It had seemed the sensible thing to do in the beginning, especially with the bank breathing down her neck about the state of her finances. But now she was confused. Damien had cleared away her outstanding debt without even blinking a reproving eye over her credit card statement. He'd also refinanced her apartment so the allowance he deposited into her account each week covered her mortgage repayments at a rate she would have had no hope of equalling unless one of her books became a top ten best-seller—which she knew wasn't likely in her lifetime. It had surprised her that he'd allowed her to keep it, but when she'd questioned him he'd informed her he had some clients who were desperate for accommodation. The hefty rent they were paying was also magically appearing in her bank account, which made her feel even more ambiguous towards him.

She wanted to feel angry at him, not grateful. Her dependence on him was increasing each day in subtle ways. Living in the same house, sharing meals and conversations with him, was making her see him in a different light. He was nothing like his more shallow brother Danny, for a start. Damien had a fine intelligence, a dry wit and a level of compassion that had taken her quite by surprise. His aloof nature, she was starting to recognise, was not just a protective device. He was a private person. Keeping his cards close to his chest was wired into his personality just as surely as Danny's outgoing party-boy image was wired into his.

Emily wished she knew why it was so important for Damien to keep his aunt's whereabouts a secret—a secret so safely guarded even his own brother didn't know. What could possibly be his reason? Was she, as rumoured, a reclusive alcoholic? Or was it something else?

Emily wandered aimlessly around Damien's house, trying to fill in the crawling minutes. Three days, he'd said. It seemed like a lifetime. The house was spotless due to the fastidious attention of Damien's housekeeper earlier that morning. Mrs Tilberry had introduced herself grudgingly and, after giving her employer's new wife an assessing glance, with a shrug of her hefty shoulders had turned and applied herself to the task of maintaining the sterile order of Damien's house. Once she'd left, Emily had gone around and deliberately shifted the sofa cushions into a more relaxed position. Then, on her way past the huge gleaming gilt-edged mirror in the dining room, she'd left a complete set of her fingerprints in one corner. She smiled mischievously at her unrepentant reflection, satisfied at last.

The mid-afternoon sunlight beckoned her outside for a long walk, the earlier heat of the day having cooled with the onset of a light coastal breeze. Emily walked for several blocks, peering into gardens and admiring the huge mansions of the exclusive leafy suburb. Her tiny apartment in the inner suburb of Stanmore seemed so pathetic compared to the grandeur surrounding her. Thinking about the way Damien had helped her keep her property made her anger towards him increasingly harder to sustain, especially now, with him absent.

His absence seemed to have multiplied her tendency to think about him. He filled her mind. It was as if he'd taken up permanent residence there, and there was now no way of evicting him. She increased her pace, determined to eradicate him from her thoughts, her feet pounding along the pavement, her head down against the playful breeze. She didn't see the woman until she cannoned into her less than half a block from Damien's house.

'Oh, I'm so sorry!' Emily reached out a steadying hand to the older woman. 'Are you all right? Did I hurt you?'

The woman grasped Emily's arm with an unsteady hand while the other went to her blue-grey hair. She looked at Emily with penetrating dark, black-button eyes.

'I'm fine. Just a wee bit shaken.' Her voice was rich with a Scottish lilt.

'I didn't see you,' Emily apologised. 'My mind was on other things and I—'

'Don't go troubling yourself,' the woman said with the hint of a rueful smile. 'I'm not very steady on my feet these days.'

'Do you have far to go?' Emily asked. 'I can walk you home if you like, to make sure you're OK?'

The woman seemed to hesitate. Emily assumed her hesitation was because the elderly were so often the target of opportunistic thieves. She smiled reassuringly at her.

'The truth is, I'm new around here. My...er...husband lives in number thirty-three. See, just there, the one with the high fence.'

The woman's eyes brightened and a smile crinkled her soft face. 'Just married, eh, lassie?'

Emily could feel herself blushing. 'Is it that obvious?'

'You've got blushing bride all over you like an Edinburgh fog.' The older woman smiled. 'So Mr Margate finally got himself a wee bride. Who'd have thought?'

'You know him?' Emily's eyes widened.

'I've not long been in Double Bay myself, but he is one neighbour I have seen now and again. He's a rather handsome lad, isn't he?'

'I... Yes, he is.' Emily blushed again, struggling a little with the Scottish accent.

'My name's McCrae,' the woman said. 'Maisie McCrae. I live in the next street.'

'I'm Emily Sher—I mean Margate.'

'So you didn't keep your own name?'

'I wasn't all that attached to it, actually,' Emily answered with honesty. 'It's really one of my stepfathers' names so I didn't mind relinquishing it.'

'Well, you've certainly married into a famous family,' Maisie said. 'He has an aunt—what's her name again?'

'Rose,' Emily offered.

'Ah, yes. Rose Margate, a fine stage actress she was in her time.'

'Yes, that's right.'

'Have you met her yet?' Maisie asked. 'She's become a recluse. No one's seen her for a wee while now.'

Emily wasn't sure how to answer. She could hardly tell Mrs McCrae that Damien had forbidden her from meeting his aunt. How would she explain that?

'I'm sure I'll get to meet her soon, Mrs McCrae,' she said after a slight hesitation. 'Damien and I have been very busy and—'

Maisie gave a tinkling laugh. 'And that's exactly how it should be when you first get married, lass. Why would a young couple want old folk around when they have each other?'

'Will you allow me to walk you home, Mrs McCrae?' Emily asked in an effort to swing the subject away from Damien.

The images in her head of her body entwined with his were already wreaking havoc on her equilibrium, especially as Mrs McCrae was quite clearly a hopeless romantic who thought all marriages were made in heaven. She wondered what the older woman would say if she told her the truth. That Damien Margate had bought her literary silence, sealing the agreement with a ring on her finger and a brand on her body that just wouldn't wash away.

'Well, that'd be nice, lass,' Mrs McCrae said, taking

Emily's arm with a tremulous hand. 'I should really be using a walking stick, but they're so ageing, don't you think?'

Emily smiled and slowed her pace to match Mrs McCrae's.

'I'm sure you can buy quite nice ones,' she offered positively.

Mrs McCrae gave her a scornful look. 'Next you'll be telling me it's not ageing to wear underwear the size of yacht sails.'

Emily burst out laughing. She hadn't laughed in so long the sensation felt strange and she quickly smothered the sound. Mrs McCrae looked at her and smiled.

'You should smile more often. You have such lovely eyes. They dance the Highland Fling when you smile.'

Emily looked away in embarrassment and they continued in a companionable silence. There was something about Mrs McCrae that appealed to her. The faltering steps beside her filled her with compassion, and she wondered if the older woman had had a stroke recently. She didn't like to ask, but pulled back her pace even more as they continued along the pathway.

Not long after they'd turned the corner Mrs McCrae stopped in front of a neat terraced house. 'This is my home. It's not as grand as its neighbours but I live alone.'

'Did you...did your husband pass away?' Emily asked uncomfortably.

'He's been long gone,' Mrs McCrae said.

'I'm sorry.'

Mrs McCrae's bright eyes twinkled again. 'Not all husbands are as irresistible as yours, my dear.'

Emily's colour returned. 'I should get going.' She took a step backwards.

'Come and visit me some time,' Mrs McCrae said. 'I don't have many visitors. We can have tea and shortbread and a good blather.'

'I'd like that,' Emily said, and gave Mrs McCrae's arm a little squeeze as she turned to walk home.

Two days later Emily was just sitting down to a snack of cheese on toast when the doorbell rang. She left her scanty evening meal and opened the front door.

'Danny! What are you doing here?'

'This is my brother's house,' Danny said, stooping to kiss her briefly on the mouth. 'While the cat's away and all that.'

Emily stepped aside as he came in, her forehead creasing into a worried frown. 'I'm not sure Damien would appreciate your sense of humour. Where's Louise?'

Danny shrugged and bent his head to smell the huge bouquet of flowers she'd put on the hall table only that morning. 'Mmm, nice.' He turned back to face her. 'Louise is visiting her mother.'

'So while the cat's away and all that?' Emily quipped darkly.

'Come on, Em, have pity on me. Let's have a drink and a chat. We're supposed to be mates, aren't we?'

'You're my brother-in-law now,' she pointed out as he strode off towards the sitting room, where the well-stocked bar was located.

'Even better,' he said, reaching for the whisky decanter. 'Damien won't mind sharing. He's used to it by now. Linda Janssen is his latest—apart from you, of course.'

Emily found his comments intensely irritating. She hated being referred to in the same sentence as Damien's mistress—it made her feel used and cheap.

Danny looked at her as he lifted his glass to his lips. 'You're not falling in love with him, are you?' he asked when she didn't speak.

Emily felt the flush rise like a tide along her cheeks. 'Of course not! You know why I married him.'

Danny's laugh was mocking. 'Yes, you married him for his money, didn't you, my sweet?'

Emily's mouth tightened. 'I wouldn't have put it quite that way,' she said.

'How would you have put it, Emily?'

Emily turned in shock at the deep sardonic sound of Damien's voice at the doorway. 'Damien!' she gasped.

Damien's brow lifted ironically. 'Surprised to see me? How touching.' He turned to his brother. 'What brings you here, Danny—apart from my wife?'

Danny finished his whisky in one mouthful. 'I thought I'd do the brotherly thing and entertain Emily for you. But since you're home now I wonder if I could speak to you about something.' He glanced briefly at Emily before adding, 'In private.'

Emily swung away to leave the room, her face set in lines of tension. She didn't trust Danny. She wondered why she hadn't seen it before, the way he inveigled himself, got what he wanted and then turned away without remorse.

'What is it this time?' she heard Damien ask as she closed the door behind her. 'Money?'

She *wouldn't* listen through the keyhole, but how she wanted to! Instead she went back to her abandoned meal and sat down and stared at the cold cheese and limp toast. Very few minutes had passed before she heard the front door slam and the roar of a car soon after.

Damien's unmistakable tread came towards the kitchen and Emily pushed her untouched food away.

'I want to talk to you,' he said as he entered the room.

Emily felt her stomach free-fall at the sheer height of him looming over her like some dark knight intent on righting the wrongs of his underlings.

'I'm having my dinner,' she said defiantly, pulling her toast back towards her.

He gave the small plate a cursory glance. 'That's not dinner—that wouldn't feed a gnat.'

'I'm not that hungry.'

'Are you upset?'

She looked up at him.

GET FREE BOOKS
and a
FREE GIFT WHEN YOU PLAY THE...

LAS VEGAS GAME

▼ DETACH AND POST CARD TODAY! ▼

Just scratch off the gold box with a coin. Then check below to see the gifts you get!

YES!
I have scratched off the gold box. Please send me my **4 FREE BOOKS** and **gift for which I qualify.** I understand that I am under no obligation to purchase any books as explained on the back of this card. I am over 18 years of age.

P4AI

Mrs/Miss/Ms/Mr _____ Initials _____

BLOCK CAPITALS PLEASE

Surname _____

Address _____

_____

Postcode _____

7	7	7	Worth FOUR FREE BOOKS plus a BONUS Gift!
🍒	🍒	🍒	Worth FOUR FREE BOOKS!
🔔	🔔	☘	TRY AGAIN!

Visit us online at
www.millsandboon.co.uk

Offer valid in the U.K. only and is not available to current Reader Service subscribers to this series. Overseas and Eire please write for details. We reserve the right to refuse an application and applicants must be aged 18 years or over. Offer expires 30th August 2004. Terms and prices subject to change without notice. As a result of this application you may receive offers from Harlequin Mills & Boon® and other carefully selected companies. If you do not wish to share in this opportunity, please write to the Data Manager at the address shown overleaf. Only one application per household.

Mills & Boon® is a registered trademark owned by Harlequin Mills & Boon Limited. The Reader Service™ is being used as a trademark.

The Reader Service™ — Here's how it works:

Accepting the free books places you under no obligation to buy anything. You may keep the books and gift and return the despatch note marked 'cancel'. If we do not hear from you, about a month later we'll send you 6 brand new books and invoice you just £2.60* each. That's the complete price - there is no extra charge for postage and packing. You may cancel at any time, otherwise every month we'll send you 6 more books, which you may either purchase or return to us - the choice is yours.

*Terms and prices subject to change without notice.

NO STAMP NEEDED!

THE READER SERVICE™
FREE BOOK OFFER
FREEPOST CN81
CROYDON
CR9 3WZ

If offer card is missing write to: The Reader Service, PO Box 236, Croydon, CR9 3RU

NO STAMP
NECESSARY
IF POSTED IN
THE U.K. OR N.I.

'Upset?'

'You told me you can't eat when you're upset. Remember?'

'Oh.' She turned back to her plate. 'No.'

'Well, I am,' he said.

She looked back at him at that. 'Because Danny was here?' she guessed.

'That and other things.'

'He's your brother. I didn't realise I was banned from speaking to him. Apart from your aunt, are there any other relatives you'd like me to keep away from?'

His expression darkened. 'Who else have you entertained while I've been away?'

She got to her feet and slammed her chair in forcibly. 'No one, although I don't see that it's any business of yours. I haven't asked for a minute-by-minute account of your time away, although no doubt it would be very enlightening.'

One of his hands snaked out and caught her arm, pulling her back to face him. 'I don't want you to spend time with Danny alone.'

'Oh?' She arched one fine brow provocatively. 'Why? Because you don't trust him? Or is it that you don't trust me?'

She suddenly found herself slammed up against him, her face far too close to his, her breasts rising and falling against the wall of hard muscle at his chest.

'I don't trust myself around you,' he ground out, 'let alone anyone else.'

She could hardly breathe but managed to ask, 'Am I to be put under lock and key?'

His dark chocolate gaze fixed on her flashing blue glare. 'No. I have other plans for you.'

'Torture?'

He gave a bitter half-smile and her stomach lurched again. 'That depends.'

'On what?' Her voice sounded breathless, husky even.

'On this,' he said, and covered her mouth with his.

It was torture, she decided some minutes later. Torture to be in his arms and know he didn't care a jot for her. They'd moved from the kitchen to the sitting room but she couldn't quite recall how. She'd locked her arms around his neck and closed her eyes as his mouth had worked its magic on hers, and when she opened them again she was being pressed to the expanse of the sofa and he was on top of her, each hard line of his very aroused body imprinting itself on hers.

His mouth moved from hers to trail a path of heat along her neck. She turned her head as he pressed soft, spine-tingling kisses along the sensitised skin, her hands tightening around his shoulders, her nails digging into his firm flesh.

'You're a wildcat,' he breathed against her mouth. 'Do you know that?'

She answered him with an open-mouthed kiss of her own, her nails digging even deeper. He returned her kiss while flames of uncontrollable desire licked along her flesh wherever his hands or fingers touched. Her clothes were a barrier that he soon dispensed with. She heard something tear and then realised it was the back of his shirt as she wrenched it out of his trousers. Two buttons flew through the air to land alongside her bra and top, and his tie coiled like a ribbon-dancer's as it joined them on the floor.

She was lost. All her determination to resist him had disappeared, replaced with a desire so strong she had no hope of turning back its tide. It was like the force of a hurricane, overtaking everything in its path, hurling reason and intellect into the swirl of relentless desire.

His hands covered her breasts, moulding their firm globes under expert fingers, tracing her sensitised nipples in tiny circles until her breath locked in her throat as he replaced his fingers in turn with his mouth. His tongue rolled over each hard nub until she thought she'd scream with her need of him. Her body arched beneath him, her pelvis melting into the strength and purpose of his.

He entered her so deeply she shuddered at the impact. He checked himself, murmured something in her ear which in her overcome state she didn't properly register. She let her body do the talking for her instead. Her legs tightened around his, her back arched to take him further, and she heard him groan as her hands raked along his back. Each movement of his body in hers brought her closer to the edge of ecstasy, only just out of reach but moving inexorably nearer. His mouth returned to hers, drawing a fiery response that left them both gasping for air.

Her cry of pleasure when it came seemed to fill the room. She bit down on his shoulder as the last of the waves rolled over and through her, and his answering groan of release was like a salve along her heated flesh.

It was a long time before either of them moved. Emily kept her eyes shut; her arms had relaxed their grip somewhat but were still around his neck. Damien's chest rose and fell rhythmically, the steady beat of his heart close to hers.

'Emily?' He shifted his body and she immediately felt empty and alone. 'Did I hurt you?'

She shook her head against his shoulder, not trusting herself to speak. He lifted himself up on one elbow to look down at her.

'I shouldn't have done that. I told myself I wouldn't.'

'It's OK.'

'No, it's not OK. It's not part of the deal.'

'Please, Damien—' She pushed against him to get up off the sofa. 'It's not a big deal. It was just sex.'

'Thanks.' His tone was resentful.

She flicked him a wry glance. 'Very good sex,' she said, stepping back into her discarded clothes.

'I thought so too,' he said as he reached for his trousers.

She had to look away.

'Have you had dinner?' she asked, plumping up the

squashed cushions on the sofa, wondering privately what Mrs Tilberry would think if she'd seen the way their bodies had just flattened them.

'No—' she heard him sigh '—you know what aeroplane food is like.'

'Can't be much worse than soggy cheese on toast.'

'Comes close, I'd say.'

She gave a reluctant smile as she turned to face him. He was looking at her intently, his dark gaze penetrating.

'When you smile your eyes dance,' he said. 'You should smile more often.'

Emily looked away, her cheeks aflame.

'What's wrong?'

'Nothing. You just reminded me of someone, that's all.'

'Who?'

'Someone I met the other day.'

'Who?'

'Your Scottish neighbour, Mrs McCrae.'

'Never heard of her,' he said dismissively.

He poured them both a drink and, handing her one, asked, 'What did Danny want?'

She took a deep sip before answering. 'We didn't get to that.'

'No.' He put his drink down. 'You were too busy discussing your motives for marrying me.'

'It wasn't quite how it sounded.'

'Oh?' His arched brow was sceptical.

'I can't see why you should be feeling affronted. You've made your own motives more than clear,' she put in.

'Have I?'

'Yes,' she said. 'I'm a smokescreen for the real love of your life. Everyone knows it.'

'Everyone?'

'Well, I know it.'

'You know nothing. You just make it up as you go along to suit yourself.'

'That's not true,' she said crossly, then, inspecting the

whisky decanter intently, added, 'Was she with you interstate?'

'Why do you want to know?'

Emily turned to look at him. 'Because I will not be made a laughing stock, that's why.'

'I wasn't with Linda,' he assured her. 'I was catching up on clients.'

She turned away again, not wanting him to see the relief on her face. 'If I'm to believe your word then you should at least believe mine.'

'Point taken,' he said, putting down his glass. 'But I still don't want Danny to visit you alone.'

'Danny is nothing to me.'

'Other than a way to gain access to my aunt.'

'I'm keeping my side of the deal,' she said. 'Even if you're not.'

His eyes moved away from hers and she felt a small sense of victory. An awkward silence fell between them. Emily finally broke it with, 'I didn't ask him to visit me.'

'Perhaps not, but you were discussing me with him.'

'Is that not allowed?'

'Absolutely not,' he insisted. 'Would you like it if I discussed what just happened between us with another party?'

'I didn't tell him anything I wouldn't have said to your face.'

'If that's supposed to reassure me, it doesn't. You've said far too much to my face as it is.'

'Only what you deserved to hear.'

'Ouch.'

'You have only yourself to blame.'

'Be that as it may, I still think you should keep away from Danny,' he said again.

'You don't like him, do you?' she asked.

'I don't trust him,' he answered. 'Any more than I trust you.'

Emily felt an inexplicable pang of hurt deep inside but covered it with a sharp barb of her own. 'That's a harsh statement from his own flesh and blood. I thought brothers stuck together through thick and thin?'

'Danny doesn't always behave like a brother,' he said, bending down to pick something up off the floor. He straightened and handed her one of her earrings, his fingers brushing hers as she took it from him. She re-inserted it into her ear lobe nonchalantly, as if nothing intimate had happened between them. She felt him watching her, her fumbling fingers betraying her façade of cool composure.

'How was your business trip, anyway?' she asked to cover her nervousness. 'Successful?'

'Nothing out of the ordinary.' He picked up his tie. 'How about you? Did you get any work done?'

'Work?'

'Aren't you working on a new book or something?'

'I...I've got writer's block.'

'So what does one usually do when such a condition strikes?' he asked.

Emily shrugged. 'Chocolate, lots of chocolate. Sometimes wine, but only when I'm really desperate.'

'Red or white?'

'Red,' she said. 'The full-bodied, headache-the-next-morning variety.'

He smiled and reached for a corkscrew in the drinks cabinet. 'Are you desperate enough for this?' He held up a gold-labelled Cabinet Savignon that she knew probably cost more than her first car.

'Not desperate,' she said. 'But tempted.'

'Good.' He deftly uncorked the bottle and reached for two crystal glasses. He poured the blood-coloured liquid and handed her one.

'Cheers,' he said, lifting his glass to chink against hers.

'What are we toasting?' she asked. 'Our paper marriage?'

His eyes glittered wryly as he took a sip of the wine.

'It's hardly a paper marriage now, is it?' he said.

Emily took a deep sip of the wine before responding.

'It's hardly a marriage. I know nothing of you; you know nothing of me.'

'I know what gives you pleasure,' he reminded her.

Emily buried her flaming face into her glass. 'I'm sure you've left a lot of very satisfied women in your wake,' she bit out tartly, 'but sexual satisfaction hardly constitutes a fulfilling relationship, let alone a marriage.'

'But it's important, surely? I mean, it would be a very stale relationship if there was no chemistry at all.' He took another sip of wine and watched the fleeting emotions on her face.

'What is it you want from me, Damien?' she asked. 'I'm getting a little mixed up over the fine print. I was under the impression this was to be a hands-off relationship, everything on paper. Wasn't that the deal?'

He put down his glass and met her fiery gaze.

'I didn't intend to sleep with you—' he began.

'You haven't slept with me!' she railed, thrusting her own glass aside. 'You just tear my clothes off when you feel like it and have sex with me. I haven't spent the night in your arms once!'

'Is that what you want?' His voice rose in frustration. 'To sleep with me? For this to be a physical marriage?'

Emily bit her lip and turned away, reaching for her glass to cover her feelings. One mouthful of good wine and she was asking for the moon. What was wrong with her?

'No,' she said determinedly. 'I just want to stick to the rules.'

'OK, then,' he said. 'I promise not to touch you. But you have to promise something to me. I want you to call your agent and tell her the book's not going to be released— ever. That it's not going to be written at all.'

'But I thought—'

'No. If that book is ever released I will sue.'

'You'd still sue me? Even though you're married to me?' she asked incredulously.

His expression hardened. 'Is that why you married me?

Did you think I wouldn't follow through? You're a good lay, I'll give you that, but I won't see my aunt's name dragged through the mud to fund your retirement, even if you are my wife.'

Emily was speechless. She stood there, the wine glass almost falling from her nerveless fingers.

'I can't believe you'd be so...so...' She struggled to find the words.

'So what, Emily?'

'So...so inhuman.'

'Who's being inhuman now? You're the one who wants to write a parcel of lies about a fragile old lady who never got a chance at happiness.'

Emily felt a wave of guilt rush through her.

'Tell me, Emily, did you ever consider the outcome of the sort of book you write?'

'I—'

'Of course you didn't,' he cut across her. 'You just sit at that computer of yours and tap away at someone's life as if it means nothing but increased sales. The more scandal, the more sales—isn't that right?'

There was nothing she could say. A lot of what he'd said was true. In the past she'd done exactly that: written anything with a hint of scandal in it to boost the interest in her work. It had definitely worked with her book about Raife Norton-Floyd, even if her own name had subsequently been dragged through the mud along with his. She'd thought by working on Rose Margate's biography she could somehow resurrect her reputation, but Damien's involvement in her life had changed all that. She was caught like a fly in a spider's web, the intricate fibres wrapping around her, tying her invisibly to him. She couldn't get away if she tried.

'Call her now,' he commanded, handing her the cordless telephone. 'Tell Clarice Connor that you've had second thoughts. Tell her anything. Unless you do I will be making my own legal moves in the morning.'

Emily took the telephone from him, her hand almost

shaking as she did so. 'I'll never get another contract,' she said desperately. 'I'll be blackballed.'

His expression was resolute. 'You're now under contract to me. Cancel the book indefinitely. I'll deal with any counter-suits personally.'

She dialled Clarice's number and waited for her to answer. The answering machine cut in after the fifth ring and Emily hesitated. Damien stood in front of her, his arms folded against his chest in an indomitable pose, and she began to speak in a cold, detached voice, as if it were not her writing career she was destroying but somebody else's.

She handed him back the telephone once she'd finished and snapped, 'Happy now?'

He put the phone back on its recharging cradle and reached for his wine. 'Once you get to know my aunt you won't regret doing that.'

'So you do intend for me to meet her some time?' she asked. 'What changed your mind? I must be a better lay than I thought.'

He frowned as he twirled the contents of his glass. 'Don't cheapen yourself like that.'

'You said it, not me.'

'I'm sorry—it was inappropriate. I was uptight and angry.'

It was a gruff apology but an apology for all that. Emily huddled herself into a corner of the sofa and sipped her wine.

'I'm going to get myself something to eat,' he said at last. 'Would you like something?'

She shook her head. 'I'm not hungry.'

He gave an exasperated sigh and left the room. Emily pushed her wine away and buried her head in her hands. How had she got herself into such a mess?

CHAPTER NINE

DAMIEN came back to the sitting room some time later with two omelettes on a tray and set them down in front of the sofa. Emily eyed the appetising food and shifted herself as far away as possible.

'Are you expecting someone?' she asked.

'No. I thought you might be hungry by now.' He handed her one of the plates and she hesitated.

'I told you, I'm not hungry.'

'Emily, you can't not eat. You're way too thin as it is. I can't have people thinking I don't feed you.'

She took the plate resentfully and poked at the omelette with the fork he'd handed her.

'It's not poisoned,' he assured her.

'I didn't think it was.'

He sat down beside her and picked up the remote control for the television.

'More wine?' he asked.

She shook her head, prodding at the food once more. She tasted a small mouthful and was surprised at how hungry she felt once she'd sampled it. A short time later the plate was empty, and she pushed it almost guiltily on to the coffee table in front of them.

'There's a good movie on the other channel.' He eyed her empty plate with approval. 'Or would you like to watch the documentary on Four?'

'I don't mind. You choose,' she said, settling back into the sofa. Her shoulders were starting to relax and her mind was becoming fuzzy from the wine she'd consumed.

Damien flipped through the channels and she stared sightlessly at the images in front of her, her mind taking her elsewhere. It was hard to see anything in her head other than the image of herself and Damien in the throes of passion together. She shifted uncomfortably in her seat and he turned briefly to look at her.

'We can watch the other channel if you'd like?' he offered.

'No—sorry—I was thinking about…about something else.'

She settled back down and forced herself to concentrate on the screen in front of her, all the while conscious of the strong male thighs within centimetres of her own. One of his arms was lying along the back of the sofa, so close to her head that if she so much as leant backwards she'd encounter his long fingers. Just knowing they were there made it torturously tempting to do so. Her head felt heavy; her neck ached with the need to lean back and be supported by the caress of his hand. She shut her eyes and concentrated on the muffled words coming from the television. If she could just think about something other than him!

She woke some time later, her eyes springing open in shock, and found herself draped across Damien's knees with one of his hands entwined in the weight of her hair.

He felt her stir and removed his hand. She sat upright and brushed at her sleepy eyes, her cheeks flushing at the way she'd virtually thrown herself across him in sleep.

'I'm sorry. I must have drifted off.'

'At least we can accurately say you've slept with me now, can't we?' he said, flicking off the TV with the remote control.

'But you weren't asleep,' she pointed out.

'No.' He brushed a fine strand of her hair out of her face as he looked at her. 'That's true.'

'Was it a happy ending?' she asked, moving out of his reach.

'What? The movie?'

She nodded.

'Happy enough, I guess.'

'You're not a romantic, then?' she asked.

'What makes you say that?'

She shrugged one slim shoulder. 'A hunch.'

'Don't measure me against other men's standards, Emily. I'm not completely without feeling.'

'I didn't suggest you were.'

'You don't like me, though, do you?' he asked.

Emily gnawed at her bottom lip, caught off guard by his question. 'Am I supposed to?'

'A few years ago you'd have been under oath to do so, but the Women's Movement put paid to that. You don't have to obey me, but I'd like to think you had some sort of respect for me.'

'Respect is earned.'

'I can see I have some work to do,' he commented wryly.

She didn't reply, but somehow his arm resting along the back of the sofa encountered her hair once more. She sat silently as his fingers threaded their way through the loose strands, her flesh tingling as he coiled the silky ends around one finger. She leant her head back to intensify the sensation of his touch and turned her head towards him, her eyes meeting his. She stared at his mouth; the firm line of his lips was relaxed into a half-smile and his hand left her hair to cup her chin.

'What am I going to do with you, Emily, wife of mine?' he asked.

Emily swallowed, not trusting herself to answer.

'You're so sweet when you're not hurling insults at me,' he mused. 'You sleep like a little child, curling up in my lap so trustingly.'

'I dribbled on your trousers.' She pointed to the damp patch on his knee in an attempt to lighten the atmosphere. The air seemed to be tightening around them, pulling them even closer than they already were.

He glanced down at his knee and smiled. 'So you did.'

Emily tried to move out of his hold but his fingers tightened fractionally on her chin.

'No, don't pull away from me. I want to talk to you.'

'You don't have to pinch my face off to do so.'

His fingers loosened, his thumb moving across to softly caress the smoothness of her cheek instead. Her breath caught in her throat at his nearness, his gentle touch stirring her blood into fervent life. His eyes locked with hers, their dark depths a whirlpool of mystery to her.

'For someone who claims to dislike me so intensely, your body insists on giving the opposite message,' he said.

'I don't know what you're talking about.'

His mouth twisted into a half-smile, his thumb moving to brush over the fullness of her bottom lip.

'Against your will, and probably against your better judgement, you really are attracted to me, aren't you?'

Emily felt cornered. 'You're rich and powerful,' she said glibly. 'Most women find that attractive. But it's a shallow sort of attraction; it won't last.'

'You seem very sure of that,' he observed, dropping his hand from her face.

'I can guarantee it. I'd give it six weeks, tops. After that the thrill of the chase fades and it all becomes a boring routine.'

'Want to put it to the test?' he challenged.

'What?'

'Let's see if your theory is true. I challenge you to spend the next six weeks with me as a proper wife.'

'You mean do your washing and ironing? Forget it! I've got better things to do with my—'

'No. You know I don't mean that. I mean sleep with me, be my lover and partner, not just on paper but in real life.'

'You can't be serious!' She got to her feet and moved agitatedly across the room.

'Of course I'm serious. I bet by the end of six weeks you won't be bored. I can guarantee it.'

'What if I am? What if you lose the bet?'

'I won't lose the bet.' His tone was confident. 'But if at

the end of six weeks you want to move on I won't stop you.'

'You mean I can leave?' She stopped and stared at him. 'Get a divorce?'

'If you feel it's necessary.'

'Of course it will be necessary. You can hardly want to spend the rest of your life tied to me any more than I want to be tied to you.'

'Let's not look too far ahead. Six weeks will do for now. As for the future, who knows?'

Emily bit her lip. This was getting way out of her control. She'd thought it was just her book she was relinquishing, but what about her heart?

'I'm not doing the cooking and cleaning,' she sniped at him. 'And I absolutely insist on sleeping on the right-hand side of the bed. I have a thing about it.'

He crossed one ankle over his knee and, leaning back into the sofa, surveyed her defiant face. 'Anything else?'

She pressed her damp palms against her thighs, wondering if she should tell him the truth. It had been months since she'd taken a birth control pill.

'Emily?'

'Yes, there is one other thing,' she said firmly. 'From now on I want you to wear a condom.'

'If you insist, but you have my assurance that during the next six weeks I will remain exclusively yours, so to speak.'

'I do insist.'

There was a tiny pause.

'And what about you, Emily?' he asked. 'Will you remain faithful to me during that time also?'

She found it difficult to meet his probing gaze.

'Naturally.'

He got to his feet and came to stand in front of her, his towering presence instantly eroding her courage.

'If you are unfaithful there will be hell to pay. You do realise that, don't you?' he asked.

Emily stood her ground even though inside her stomach had turned to jelly at the light of warning shining in his eyes.

'I realise you want to make me suffer as much as possible, and won't let any opportunity pass that affords you the chance to do so,' she said valiantly.

'Your opinion of me seems to be disintegrating more each day,' he reflected ruefully. 'Who knows what it will be at the end of six weeks?'

'I can tell you now,' she said. 'I'll still loathe and detest you.'

His sardonic laugh irritated her beyond belief.

'Are you sure, sweet Emily?' His hand caught her up-tilted chin once more, forcing her defiant eyes to meet his. 'Don't go staking your life on it, now, will you?'

She ground her teeth and pulled out of his grasp.

'You'd just love it if I fell at your feet in lovelorn worship, wouldn't you? But it's just not going to happen. You're everything I most dislike in a man. You're arrogant, controlling and have an ego the size of a continent.'

'You're not quite my idea of a perfect partner yourself,' he bit back. 'Since we're trading insults: you're a promiscuous little madam who'd do anything for a good story. You've already proved it by hooking up with Danny, only to discard him to marry me because you thought it would throw you directly into Rose's path. But your little scheme didn't work, did it?'

'Marriage was your idea, not mine.'

'But it played right into your desperate little hands, didn't it? I was wondering just how far you'd go and you did exactly as I expected. You sold your soul for money, my money. I heard you confess as much to Danny.'

There was nothing she could say in her own defence.

'No come-back to flay me with?' he taunted. 'No witty pay-back to put me firmly in my place?'

'I wouldn't waste my breath,' she spat at him.

The telephone rang shrilly on the side table and Damien

reached out a long arm to answer it. He spoke into it briefly before handing it to her. 'It's for you.'

Emily took the telephone receiver and turned her back on him. 'Hello?'

'What the hell do you mean, you're pulling *Rose's Cupboard* from the drawing-board?' Clarice Connor's voice carried across the room. 'You can't do that!'

Emily took a deep breath. 'I just did.'

'Emily, you can't be serious! Is this some sort of publicity stunt? I mean, marrying the nephew was good, so good that everyone wants the book! I've had everyone on my back for the past week, crying out for a date of completion. You can't withdraw your proposal now.'

'I have to.'

'Who says? This is the big break we've been waiting for. You can't afford to let this go. Damn it! *I* can't afford to let this go.'

'This is about me, not you, Clarice,' Emily said. 'I'm not writing it. I've got no other choice.'

'Well, I'm quitting as your agent,' Clarice said. 'I'm not putting up with this any longer. I'm losing all credibility because of you. No one will want to be represented by me after this.'

'I'm sorry, Clarice, but—'

'You're sorry?' Clarice's tone was scathing. 'I'm sorry I ever took pity on you in the first place. I should've known after that Norton-Floyd affair you'd be nothing but trouble. I suppose the lure of the Margate millions has swayed you, has it? I never would've thought it of you. I never thought you'd sell yourself so cheaply.'

Emily flinched as Clarice hung up on her. She was very conscious of Damien's silent presence behind her as she clutched the buzzing receiver to her chest.

She felt his hand on her shoulder, and his voice when he spoke was deep but gentle. 'Give me the phone, Emily.'

She handed it to him, her hands not quite steady. He put

the receiver back in its cradle and faced her. 'I realise this has cost you, but believe me it's for the best.'

'Best for whom?' she asked bitterly. 'For you?'

'For Rose.'

She brushed at the moisture in her eyes, angry that he was witnessing her professional humiliation.

'I'll be waiting on café tables for the rest of my life. No one will want to take me on after this—no one.'

'That's not true,' he assured her. 'You can change direction—write something else.'

'You make it sound so easy.' She sniffed. 'As if I could walk out there and tap the nearest agent on the shoulder now and say, "Take me on. I've had one success, one disaster, and I pulled the plug on my last one, but I'll try and get it right this time." As if!'

'What did you do before you wrote your first book?'

'I was a cadet on a local newspaper. I was propositioned by the chief editor once too many times and left.'

'You should have taken him to court.'

'With whose money?' she asked. 'And who would've believed me?'

'What drew you to write about my aunt?'

Emily sat back down and took the wine glass he'd refilled and handed to her.

'I'm not sure. I guess it was the mystery of it all that grasped my attention. Here was a woman with the world at her feet and suddenly she disappeared, never to be seen again. No explanation, no farewell. Just silence.'

'It was her choice.'

'I realise that, but it didn't make sense. Why throw away all that fame for obscurity? What possible reason could there be for such a dramatic turnaround?'

'People have their reasons,' he said. 'Fame isn't all it's cracked up to be. Some of the most popular celebrities can also be the loneliest.'

Emily sipped her wine and thought about his words.

'Many people, such as yourself, have concluded Rose

has become a reclusive alcoholic, but I can assure you that's not true.'

'If she would just give one interview, the gossip would go away and—'

'No.' His tone was adamant. 'I won't allow it.'

'You won't allow it? But what about what Rose wants?'

'I speak to Rose every couple of days. I know exactly what she wants.'

Emily got to her feet and put her half-finished wine on the table. 'I think I'll go to bed now,' she informed him curtly. 'I'm tired.'

'I'll be up in a few minutes,' he said, draining his glass.

She hesitated. 'Do...do you want me to—?'

'Yes,' he said emphatically, his eyes burning into hers. 'I do want you.'

She left the room on unsteady legs, her heart thumping in her chest. What had she agreed to? Six weeks of pleasure for what price? Her peace of mind or her heart?

She turned to the big bed and slipped in beneath the covers, burrowing herself into a tight ball. The linen smelt of his aftershave and she suppressed a tiny shiver of apprehension as she curled into the nearest pillow, willing her eyelids to close in instant slumber.

No chance. She tossed and wriggled, trying to find a comfortable spot in the huge bed, but it was impossible for her to relax. The light coming from downstairs annoyed her. The firmness of the pillow annoyed her. The thought of Damien joining her terrified her. How could she hold back her response to him? As much as she claimed to detest him, her body had other ideas. It craved him. Even now, in anticipation of him joining her in the big bed, she could feel the betraying moisture pooling in secret. Within minutes he would reach for her, his own body ready, poised for possession, and she would have no choice but to respond to its urge.

She clamped her eyes shut when she heard his footsteps.

She turned her back and rolled into a tight little ball, willing herself to ignore the opening of the door; fighting against the desire to spring out of bed and escape to the other room, safe from the temptation of his touch. Her chest felt tight with the effort of controlling her erratic breathing. She felt like screaming, but still she lay silent, all her senses on full alert, waiting, both dreading but craving his presence in the bed beside her.

She felt the depression of the mattress as he lay down. He readjusted the pillow under his head with an audible grunt and she felt one of his legs touch hers as he stretched out his length. She held her breath, tensely poised in readiness for his hands reaching for her.

'You can relax, Emily,' he said as he pulled the covers towards him. 'I'm bushed and so are you.'

Emily let her breath out gradually. She lay in the dark and listened to his steady breathing, hardly daring to move in case she stirred him.

'By the way—' she felt him turn towards her '—you're lying on my side of the bed. It was the right side you were so particular about, wasn't it?'

'I...it doesn't matter,' she said lamely, burrowing down amongst the pillows, pulling the covers back over her skimpy nightwear.

'Good,' he said. 'Because I'm too tired to fight you for it, but, believe me, if I wasn't I'd win, hands down.'

Emily didn't argue. She simply curled even more tightly on the left-hand side of his bed and shut her eyes, willing herself to oblivion.

It was impossible for her to sleep. She lay there fuming that he could drop off so easily while she was tossing and twitching with tension. How dare he? Wasn't he the least bit affected by her lying next to him? She turned her pillow over one more time, laying her head back down on the cooler linen, but within minutes it again felt too warm for comfort. She considered getting up to open a window but didn't want to risk waking him.

She sneaked a look at him in the soft glow of the moonlight but he appeared to be sleeping soundly. His face was relaxed. Gone were the deep lines of tension that had earlier been etched around his mouth. Emily wondered what sort of worries put them there. She realised with a pang of shame she'd asked him nothing of his work, what pressures he had to cope with each day. All she'd done was fight with him and try to get the upper hand.

She sighed and lay back to stare sightlessly at the ceiling. She wondered what it would be like to be really married to him. Not just on paper, and not just because he wanted to stop her writing her book, but because he wanted to spend the rest of his life with her. She wondered what it would feel like to be loved so much, to have someone to lean on through life's difficult passages, someone who'd always be there to talk to.

She shut her eyes against the sting of tears. Was it so much to ask to be loved? Especially when her life had always short-changed her in that department? She thought of her father, who'd left when she was four; and of her mother who'd been unable to cope and had taken out her rejection and hurt on Emily and her brothers. Her various stepfathers had joined her mother's mission of bitterness against her children. Emily's childhood had been about survival, not love.

She had read somewhere how unmet needs in childhood could influence some of the mistakes adults make in later life. Marrying Damien had been one of those mistakes, but she could see now why she'd done it. For so many years she'd lived on her wits, alone and struggling to keep her head above water. Damien had offered her a solution and she'd jumped at it, not thinking of the long-term implications of such an arrangement. She hadn't even stopped to give thought to protecting herself from pregnancy, which was an ever-increasing worry in the back of her mind. She couldn't imagine what Damien would say if she were to tell him of her suspicions. He'd no doubt accuse her of setting him up for child maintenance, believing her to have deliberately orchestrated it to ensure a steady income for herself for the next eighteen or so years.

She felt sick. A wave of panic swept over her. Surely it was too early for morning sickness?

'Will you stop wriggling and kicking me in the shins?' Damien growled beside her, startling her out of her wretched reverie. His arms came around her, and before she could speak he lifted her over himself and repositioned her on the right-hand side of the bed, where his body had just been lying. 'There, is that better?'

Emily was still lying in the circle of his arms, his long legs entwined intimately with hers.

'Yes,' she croaked.

'Good.' He shifted slightly and she felt the unmistakable heat of his arousal against her. 'It feels much better for me too.'

His mouth came down and covered hers, his arms pulling her even closer to the warmth of his body. Emily sighed and opened her mouth to the urge of his tongue, her smooth thighs sliding apart to allow him to settle between them with his pressing need.

What was the point in crying for the moon when at least she had this paradise in his arms, even if it was only for another six weeks? Some people spent their lifetime without ever experiencing the completeness she felt as Damien's lover.

Damien's lover. How strange that sounded to her ears. She was his lover, and she loved him. There was no point denying it to herself any longer. She didn't know quite how it had started; perhaps that first night when he'd tried to keep Danny's perfidy away from her by accompanying her to the awards night. Or maybe it had been on the evening of their wedding day when he'd tended her injured hand with hands so gentle it had made her cry. Or was it because of this pleasure she was feeling even now in his arms? This mindless, frantic, all-encompassing pleasure that rocketed through her body in waves so strong she wondered if she would faint with the sheer sensuality of it all.

CHAPTER TEN

EMILY woke up alone. There was a note on the pillow next to her face. She sat up and, pushing the curtain of hair out of her eyes, began to read it.

> *Emily,*
> *I have an early meeting. Some delegates from the firm are arriving from interstate. There's a dinner scheduled for this evening. I'd like you to be there. I'll pick you up at seven. D.*

Emily stared at the strong handwriting, the clipped, efficient words that bore no resemblance to the passion and intimacy they'd shared just hours earlier.

She sighed. Fool! she remonstrated with herself as she flung back the bed covers. What had she been expecting? A declaration of undying love? She stubbed her toe on the bedside table and swore. Tears welled in her eyes, not from the pain in her foot but from the empty ache in her heart.

The telephone was ringing as she stepped out of the shower and she hastily draped a towel over her dripping body to answer it.

'Emily? It's Maisie McCrae.'

Emily clutched the slipping towel and tried to cover the surprise in her voice. 'How are you, Mrs McCrae? I was going to visit you, but I thought—'

'Please call me Maisie,' she said. 'I was wondering if you had anything planned for today?'

'No, nothing.' Then, remembering Damien's note, added, 'I do—I mean we have a dinner on tonight, but I'm free all day.'

'A romantic dinner for two?'

'No. It's a work thing.'

'You sound disappointed,' Maisie said.

Emily didn't know how to answer.

'Well, I didn't phone you to talk about your husband,' Maisie continued, regardless. 'I phoned because I was hoping you could visit me today.'

'I'd like that,' Emily said, thinking of the long, empty day ahead. 'I'd like that very much.'

Maisie came to the door dressed in a dark blue trouser suit that looked comfortable rather than fashionable. Her thick blue-grey hair was tied back with a scarf and her pale face was unadorned except for a soft pink lipstick. She gasped in pleasure at the bunch of flowers Emily had brought her.

'How delightful.' She buried her face in the bouquet before turning to her with a smile. 'I haven't been given flowers for years. Come in and sit down. I'll make us some tea.'

Emily followed her into the neat sitting room off the hall. The view over Double Bay and out across to Point Piper was breathtaking.

'How beautiful!' she exclaimed, going to the window.

'I sit and look out there for hours,' Maisie said. 'I'm sure if I didn't have such a marvellous view I wouldn't be quite the hermit I've become.'

Emily turned to look at her. There was something about Maisie that was different. She couldn't quite put her finger on it, but she sensed it all the same.

'Are you really a hermit?'

Maisie sighed and handed her a china tea cup.

'Some would describe it as such. I suppose some would even say I've become agoraphobic, but I don't see it that way. If I have to go out I will, but I don't choose to unless it's absolutely necessary. I don't like people staring at me, wondering what's wrong with me.'

Emily lowered her gaze and concentrated on the border

of roses running along the rim of the cup in her hand. 'Have you had a stroke?' she asked gently.

'No.' Maisie answered. 'I've got Parkinson's Disease.'

Emily's eyes sought the older woman's. 'I'm so sorry. It must be difficult for you.'

'I manage,' Maisie said. 'But enough about me. What do you do? Do you still work now that you're married? I don't suppose you have to with that rich husband of yours.'

'I used to be a writer,' she said despondently.

'Used to be?'

'I've been dumped by my agent. I had some trouble over my latest project.'

'Tell me about it.'

Emily hesitated briefly before confessing, 'I was all set to write a biography on...someone famous, but a relative put the brakes on.'

'Oh, really?'

'I couldn't risk being sued. I was up to my eyeballs in debt anyway. I took the easy way out instead.'

'What was the easy way out?'

Emily found it hard to meet the other woman's eyes. 'I accepted a pay-out.'

'A generous one?'

'From some angles, yes.'

'But not yours?'

Emily put the cup she was cradling down.

'I don't know what to think any more,' she said. 'Sometimes I think he—' she checked herself '—the relative was right. It must be hard to be in the public eye all the time. The person I was writing about decided to remove herself from it for whatever reason. I guess she had the right to do so. But then, how can such a celebrity turn her back on the very people who put her on the public pedestal in the first place?'

Maisie sipped her tea thoughtfully before responding. 'It's a difficult choice. I suppose it's one of priorities and motivations. People have their reasons for their actions. We might not always agree, but each of us has to do what is right for us at the time.'

'Yes, I guess you're right,' Emily said. 'I just wish I could meet her and get to know her as a person.'

'I take it you're referring to your husband's aunt?'

Emily privately marvelled at Maisie's perception.

'Yes.'

'No doubt she'll want to meet you eventually,' Maisie reassured her.

'Not as yet.'

'Give it time,' Maisie said. 'You've only been married a short time, lass. Things can change.'

'I certainly hope so,' Emily said.

'You're not happy, are you, dear?'

She shifted uncomfortably under the black-button gaze. 'I find happiness elusive at times.'

'Do you love your husband?'

'Yes.'

Maisie seemed satisfied with her answer and passed her a plate of shortbread. Emily took one and bit into it absently as she thought about what she'd just confessed to. Every breath she took was to keep her alive until the next time she was in his arms.

'You seem a little troubled, Emily,' Maisie said.

Emily lifted her distracted gaze to the woman in front of her. Maisie was looking at her intently, her probing gaze threatening to see through to the very fibres of her soul.

'I'm a little on edge,' Emily admitted at last. 'Because I think my husband's having an affair.'

Maisie examined the tea leaves in her cup before putting it down with a trembling hand.

'What makes you think that?' she asked.

'I've been told.'

'You can't believe everything you've been told,' Maisie said. 'Sometimes you have to learn to trust.'

'I don't know what to do,' Emily said desperately. 'I

haven't loved anyone since I was four years old. What am I supposed to do?'

Maisie took one of Emily's hands in her own and began to stroke it soothingly, her dark, intent eyes holding hers.

'Tell your husband how you feel.'

'I can't do that.' Emily lifted her tortured gaze to Maisie's.

'Why?'

'Because he...' She abandoned her sentence and stared once more at the rim of roses around her cup.

'Just be yourself,' Maisie said after a long silence. 'He couldn't possibly fail to love you. Just allow him to see you for who you really are.'

The pattern of roses beneath Emily's gaze blurred. What was it about Maisie McCrae that saw through to her very soul? How had this old lady seen through her carefully constructed disguise of worldliness and I-don't-give-a-damn attitude?

She hunted for a tissue under her sleeve to no avail.

'Here.' A soft pink tissue appeared as if by magic in her hand. 'I'm a great believer in tears. God knows, I've cried enough of them in my lifetime.'

Emily sobbed into the quickly drenched tissue. She blew her nose and tried to get herself under some sort of control. 'I never cry,' she gulped. 'I hate crying. Once I start I can't stop.'

'I understand.'

'Do you?' Emily lifted her face from the shield of her hands. 'Do you really?'

Maisie McCrae nodded.

'I've cried buckets over the years about all the things I should have done but didn't. About all the things I did but shouldn't have.'

Emily sensed a wealth of wisdom behind the older woman's words.

'What have you regretted the most?' she asked, scrunching up the sodden tissue in her hand.

Maisie looked at her for a long moment.

'I wish I hadn't fallen in love with the wrong man. If only that hadn't happened so many people's lives wouldn't have been affected.'

'Your husband?'

Maisie shook her head. 'I'm afraid not.'

'Oh.' Emily looked at her hands.

'Life doesn't always go according to plan,' Maisie said. 'It has a habit of twisting and turning when you least expect it.'

'Yes, I know.'

'Tell me about your family,' Maisie said.

Emily tensed. 'My father left when I was four.'

'And?'

'My mother remarried four times. Each time her choice was worse than the previous one.'

'And?'

'And I hated all of them.'

'Why?'

'Because they didn't love me for who I was.'

'That's very important to you, isn't it, Emily?'

'Yes.'

'Even after all these years it still matters to you what people think of you?'

'Doesn't everyone worry about that?' Emily asked.

'Only the very insecure worry about what others think,' she said. 'Those who are truly happy in their own skins don't give a damn.'

Emily picked up her tea cup and pretended to drink the remaining dregs. She was beginning to think Maisie McCrae saw far too much.

'I have to tell you something,' Maisie said after a small silence.

Emily scrubbed at the last of her tears and lifted her gaze to the dark intense one opposite.

'My name isn't Maisie McCrae,' she said with absolutely no trace of a Scottish lilt. She lifted a hand to her head and, to Emily's amazement, removed the grey hair to reveal dark curls lightly peppered with silver. 'I'm Damien's aunt, Rose Margate.'

Emily gaped at the other woman in shock, her tea cup clattering into its saucer. Rose had the grace to look a little shamefaced.

'I wanted to be certain I could trust you before I told you who I was.'

Emily's mind raced back and forth as she came to grips with Rose's revelation. She retraced their previous conversation and began to put the pieces together.

'I thought there was something vaguely familiar about you,' Emily finally managed. 'You seemed to be able to see things no one else has seen.'

'I only saw what you allowed me to see,' Rose said. 'What you should have shown Damien weeks ago.'

'It's too late,' Emily said, her heart sinking in despair. 'It's far too late.'

'There are things about Damien you should know,' Rose said. 'Damien is not Danny's real brother. Their father, my brother Donald, had an affair. Damien was the product of that relationship, and because Cora had been unable to have a child she agreed to bring him up as her own. Not long after, she fell pregnant with Danny. I have reason to believe Danny isn't Donald's offspring. Cora was bitter about his earlier affair and decided on her own little pay-back.'

'Oh, my God!' Emily sagged in her chair. No wonder Damien hadn't wanted her snooping around for information with those sorts of secrets in the family vault! Her heart squeezed tightly at the thought of his painful childhood, not all that dissimilar from her own.

'Does Danny know about this?' Emily asked.

Rose shook her head. 'No, he was never told the details. Damien overheard a bitter argument between his parents and came to me for advice. We've always been close.'

'Does Damien know who his real mother is?'

'He hasn't pursued it. It would've drawn too much attention to the Margate name. I left the theatre in the middle of a season. I'd been feeling the tremors for months, and I didn't consider myself so much of a brilliant actress that I could pass off as a person in full health. I didn't want people to point and comment on how much I'd deteriorated. I couldn't bear it.'

'I'm so sorry,' Emily said. 'I should never have planned to write about you.'

'I don't hold it against you, dear. I deliberately set out to meet you that day, you know. I'd hoped the accent and wig would keep me undercover until I got to know you.'

'You were very convincing,' Emily confirmed. 'But I did have this feeling I'd met you before.'

'Donald, Damien's father, and I were twins. The Margate family likeness is very strong. That's why I wear a wig in public. I've not long come down from the country. Damien provided a safe rural haven for me for years, but recently I decided to move closer to medical help. I'd appreciate it if you'd keep my whereabouts a total secret.'

'Of course I will.'

'Tell no one you've met me. Not even Damien, and especially not Danny.'

'Why not Damien?' Emily asked.

Rose thought about it for a long moment before answering.

'I think he needs some more time to get to know you. The real you.'

After leaving Rose's, Emily caught a bus to Bondi Junction instead of going back to Damien's house. She needed some time to think. Rose Margate had completely surprised her. It was ironic, really. The celebrated actress had given the performance of her life and she, Emily Sherwood-Margate, had fallen for it hook, line and sinker. She hadn't even recognised the subject of the book she wanted to write because the subject of her book was still, after all these years, a phenomenal actress.

Emily couldn't help smiling ruefully as she stepped on the bus. The Scottish accent had fooled her. How hadn't she seen through it? The Margate likeness was so obvious now she was aware of it. The black-button eyes, the determined chin, the penetrating stare...

Emily wanted to find something to wear for the dinner that evening, as well as squeezing in a hair appointment, and she forced herself to put her mind to the task. She didn't want to think about Damien or his aunt. Doing so reminded her of her own part in adding to the pain of their lives. How Damien must hate her for what she'd tried to do! No wonder he'd been so determined to buy her silence.

It was close to six p.m. when she returned to the house, where she encountered Damien in a foul mood.

'Where the hell have you been?' he roared at her as soon as she stepped through the door.

She put her bags down and tucked an escaping strand of hair behind her ear. 'I went shopping.'

'All day?'

Emily blinked.

'I've been calling you since ten o'clock this morning. I thought something must have happened to you,' he continued crossly.

'Well, no doubt you're disappointed, but here I am alive and well,' she said archly.

'You should've called me.'

'On what number?' She glared back at him. 'I've only been to your office once and I have no idea what number to call.'

'I'm sorry.' He raked a hand through his hair. 'You're right, of course.' He reached for the jacket of his suit, which he'd hung on the banister of the stairs. He took out a business card from his wallet and handed it to her.

She gave it a cursory glance before slipping it into her purse.

'Well, now I'll know who to call if I need financial advice.' She brushed past him to go upstairs. 'Excuse me, I have to get changed.'

'Emily.'

She stalled on the first step, turning to face him.

He looked at her, clutching her shopping bags under one slim arm, her eyes sparkling with defiance, her beautiful honey-coloured hair defying the lotions and potions of expert application to cascade at random about her shoulders.

'Never mind,' he said, turning away. 'I'll wait for you in the lounge.'

Emily turned back and bolted up the stairs.

She came back down forty minutes later dressed in a calf-length cerulean sheath with tiny shoestring straps that emphasised the slimness of her shoulders and the gentle curve of her breasts. Her hair was still mostly on top of her head, apart from a few wayward tendrils that insisted on caressing her shoulders.

Damien's eyes travelled over her appreciatively as she stood before him. 'You look beautiful,' he said.

'Thank you.'

He opened the door for her and she walked through, conscious of his eyes following her every movement.

The journey in the car was painfully silent. Emily framed several sentences in her head but it never seemed quite the right moment to speak. He was either concentrating on traffic or on the issue of where to park, so in the end she remained silent.

He finally parked between two cars, not far from the restaurant in Neutral Bay. He opened her door for her and casually took her arm as they walked along the pavement towards the restaurant.

'Every three months or so the interstate partners in the firm get together and run through various practice matters. These evening functions are a way for the wives—or husbands, as the case may be—to socialise. I hope you won't find it too boring.'

'I'll try and make the best of it,' she said, sneaking a glance at him.

He looked down at her and seemed about to say something when a couple stepped from a car just ahead of them. A booming voice greeted them.

'Damien, my man! And this must be your charming bride.' A huge paw grasped Emily's hand and shook it vigorously. Another strand of her hair fell down at the impact and Damien slipped an arm around her shoulders and pulled her gently towards him.

'Darling,' he said, sending a shiver up her spine at his casually delivered endearment. 'This is Hugo Brand and his wife Jeanne. This is Emily.'

Jeanne pressed a cold fish hand into Emily's while Hugo looked on beamingly.

'Never thought you'd get around to it, Damo.' He grinned. 'Just wait till you get a couple of kids running around your feet. You won't know what hit you.'

Emily fought against the blush she could feel stealing along her cheeks but fortunately Damien was looking elsewhere. She looked up to follow the line of his gaze and watched as another couple approached them. The man was tall and blond, with the sort of Scandinavian good looks that always drew female stares. The woman was attractive also. Not quite as tall as the man, and a deep brunette with the sort of figure most women had to pay for.

'Damien,' the woman said, reaching up to kiss both his cheeks. 'You look scrumptious.'

'Now, now, Linda.' The blond man chuckled. 'The man's got a wife.'

'Andre and Linda Janssen.' Damien pushed Emily forward. 'This is Emily, my wife.'

Emily didn't know how she got through it. Her hand went out and touched each of theirs briefly, and her face smiled as if she were really delighted to meet them both, but on the inside she was crumbling.

So this was Linda Janssen, his mistress. Andre didn't

look the type to turn a blind eye, but then, Emily thought, Linda didn't look the type to be playing up either. She gave the impression she adored her husband, holding on to his arm as they made their way to the restaurant door, smiling up at him when he joked with Damien about the day's meetings. Emily trailed along on Damien's arm, feeling terribly out of place. The mouse-like Jeanne followed in Hugo's wake, looking too shy to say boo to a goose. It was going to be a long evening.

The food was beautifully presented and arrived at exactly the right intervals along with the best of wines, both red and white, but later Emily could barely recall what she'd eaten, and she didn't drink at all, other than to sip at a tall glass of iced water.

At some point during the dinner Damien turned to her with the bottle of red wine in his hand. 'Drink, darling?' he asked.

'No, thank you.' Her eyes flashed at him. 'Darling.'

He reached beyond her to pass the bottle to Hugo, who took it with gusto, filling his own empty glass.

'Damien tells me you're a writer,' Hugo said, swivelling his huge bulk towards her. 'I've never met a real-life writer before.'

'It's not as glamorous as it sounds, believe me,' she said.

Linda leaned across Jeanne to address Emily. 'Is it true about the book you were going to write being cancelled?'

Several heads turned their way.

'Yes.' Emily flicked a glance in Damien's direction before continuing. 'I was given another offer too good to refuse. I decided to take it. The compensation so far has been adequate, although it may yet prove to be a foolish move on my part.'

'Sounds intriguing.' Linda reached for her wine. 'Are you working on another book now?'

'No, nothing at the moment,' she said. 'I'm considering a career change.'

'Oh? What will you do?' Linda asked.

'I haven't decided as yet. I'm still considering my options.'

'That's the trouble with women these days, Damo.' Hugo leant across Emily, breathing wine fumes over her. 'They're too damned intelligent. Whatever happened to the women who wanted nothing more than a brood of kids and some housekeeping money once a week?'

Emily let Linda and Jeanne do the protesting for her. The spirited discussion carried on without her, while her mind was engaged elsewhere.

At last it was over. Linda and Andre were the first to make a move and Damien stood up with them, reaching for Emily's hand.

'Come on, darling,' he said, looking down at her. 'You look ready for bed.'

'Damien!' Linda scolded him. 'You're making the poor girl blush.'

Emily bore it with good grace, although she was determined to give Damien an earful once they were alone. Hugo and Jeanne followed them out of the restaurant and left them to walk to Damien's car alone.

Emily walked beside him, pulling her hand out of his once the others had left.

'Wasn't the food to your liking?' Damien asked as he deactivated the central locking of his Jaguar. 'You didn't seem to be eating much.'

He opened the door for her and she slipped in under his arm, avoiding his eyes.

'I wasn't particularly hungry,' she said once he joined her in the car.

'You shouldn't let people like Hugo upset you.' He looked across at her as he turned the engine over. 'He's a harmless old bear.'

'I wasn't upset by Hugo.'

He drove towards the Harbour Bridge, his attention on the merging traffic. She waited for him to ask what had upset her but he remained silent.

'Aren't you going to ask?' she snapped at him after some time had passed.

He glanced at her briefly before checking the mirrors to change lanes. 'Ask what?'

She fumed, clenching her hands into tight fists in her lap. 'Why I'm upset, of course!'

'I would've thought that was more than obvious,' he commented wryly. 'You found spending an evening in my company utterly deplorable, didn't you?'

Emily ground her teeth and bit out, 'No, actually, what I found deplorable was having to spend the evening sitting opposite your mistress.'

'You still seem rather convinced of that old story. But tell me, did you happen to notice her husband sitting beside her all evening?' he asked.

'That means nothing. You were sitting beside me all evening and it didn't stop Linda from flirting with you.'

'Now you're being ridiculous.' His tone was impatient.

'Tell me you don't have a special relationship with her,' she demanded. 'Go on. Tell me.'

'I'm not going to allow this conversation to continue,' he said, taking the Double Bay exit. 'You're not being rational and I'm getting angry.'

'Oh, good!' she taunted. 'The aloof Damien Margate is about to explode with uncontrollable emotion. What fun this will be.'

'Careful, Emily,' he warned. 'You might not like the consequences.'

He pulled into the driveway and she got out as soon as he stopped the car. He called her, but she continued to make her way to the house regardless. It was only when she reached the front door that she realised she didn't have her key.

He came up behind her and unlocked the door over her shoulder, propelling her through with his other hand. He turned her to face him, the front door closing heavily under the thrust of his hand.

'I don't want to hear you speak of Linda Janssen in such a way again. Is that clear?'

Emily lifted her chin a fraction, her blue eyes refusing to be intimidated by his. 'Why?' she challenged him. 'Does it make you feel guilty?'

He reined in his temper with an effort. 'I won't tell you again.'

'What are you going to do Damien—darling?' she goaded him recklessly. 'Take me to court?'

'No,' he said, reaching for her before she could step away. 'I'm going to take you to bed.'

CHAPTER ELEVEN

SHE should have fought him. She should have resisted his mouth and hands. But she didn't. As soon as his lips ground against hers in a bruising kiss she was instantly caught up in a maelstrom of passion that had only one sure end. She returned his kiss with a blistering heat of her own, her tongue tangling with his, her legs threatening to give way beneath her as he crushed her to him.

One of the pictures hanging behind her wobbled precariously as their surging bodies collided with it in their haste. Damien steadied it with one hand while the other pushed aside one of Emily's shoestring straps to gain access to her breast. She gasped as his hand shaped her, his thumb grazing a path over her engorged nipple as his mouth returned to hers.

She was sure he was going to take her then and there on the stairs. She was mentally preparing herself for it when he scooped her up in his arms and carried her to his bedroom, tipping her on to his bed and coming down on top of her, his mouth still hard upon hers.

Emily tore at his shirt with greedy fingers. His belt buckle was digging into her stomach so she removed it from his waist, flinging it to one side of the bed. Her fingers sought the zip of his trousers without shame, releasing it with a gasp of anticipation as his erection brushed against her hand. She held him, shaping him with exploring fingers, her heart leaping in her chest at the dark light of desire burning in his gaze as he looked down at her.

'There's a condom in the bedside table drawer,' he said huskily. 'You can put it on for me.'

She fumbled in the drawer and unpeeled the wrapper.

She took her time, enjoying the power she had over him as he groaned at her feather-light touch, until he could stand it no more and pushed her back down on the mattress, pinning her with his strong thighs.

'Tell me you want me,' he demanded, nudging her intimately with his body.

'I want you.' She stared with unashamed longing at him.

He pushed her dress upwards, his gaze raking her boldly from the flat plane of her stomach to the tiny triangular lace that barely covered her. He hooked a finger under the lace and pulled it away, uncovering her femininity, his eyes feasting on her perfect form.

She held her breath as his mouth started at her belly button, trailing downwards until she could feel his warm breath on her intimately.

'Oh, God,' she gasped as his tongue separated her, toying with her until she was writhing with a pleasure so intense it was almost like pain. She let out a cry, a soft whimpering cry that rose and rose until she had to bite down on her bottom lip to stop herself from screaming out loud.

He slid back over her and entered her deeply, his own groan of need also sounding loud in the silence of the night. 'You feel so damn good,' he said against her mouth. 'So unbelievably good.'

Emily could feel her pleasure building all over again with each deep surge of his body inside hers, bringing her towards new heights of feeling. Her body was soaring, all her tense muscles turning into molten liquid by the touch of his hands.

He timed it perfectly. Just as she was being swept away by another tide of earth-shattering sensuality his own release sounded in her ear: a deep guttural groan that sent shivers trickling through her, increasing her own pleasure with its heavy pulse.

He rolled away and, breathing heavily, lay with one arm flung across his eyes. Emily wriggled out of the remains of her dress and, picking up the nearest bathrobe, disappeared into the *en suite* bathroom.

She showered and brushed her teeth, stalling for time. She hoped he'd be asleep by the time she came out. Her passionate reaction to him embarrassed her; she was supposed to hate him but he had only to touch her and she was aflame. It made her feel far too vulnerable, as if he had the upper hand and she was just a pawn in his game.

She came out of the *en suite* bathroom to find him sitting up against the pillows on her side of the bed, leafing through a book. He put it down as she approached the bed, his expression slightly mocking.

'Washing all trace of my detestable presence away, Emily?'

Emily straightened her spine and met the satirical glitter in his eyes. 'You're on my side of the bed.'

'Am I?' He put his hands behind his head in a make-me-move pose.

'You know you are.' She stood at the end of the bed and glared at him. 'You're doing it deliberately to annoy me.'

'Why don't you come and push me back to where I belong?' he challenged her. 'It could be fun.'

'You've had your fun. Now move over.'

'Now, now, let's be fair. You had your fun too.' His mouth curled upwards in a sardonic smile. 'I made sure of that.'

Emily felt the colour of her shame rise from the very soles of her feet to pool in her cheeks like fans of fire.

'Don't be embarrassed, my sweet,' he said. 'It's nothing to be ashamed of, this chemistry we have together. Who knows? You might not even be bored after six months with me.'

'I'd never survive that long. I'd kill myself.'

He laughed and she tore her eyes away from the ripple of muscle along his abdomen, the sheet he'd pulled over his legs doing little to disguise his nakedness.

'So dramatic,' he teased. 'Come on, hop into bed and

get some sleep. You look like a child who's been kept up too late—all eyes and pouty lips.'

She clenched her fists and, moving to the head of the bed, flicked the sheet back angrily. She lay down stiffly, turning her back on him, keeping herself as far away from the warmth and temptation of his long muscular body as possible.

She felt the brush of his fingers along the base of her spine and shivered.

'Come closer,' he said temptingly. 'I want to kiss you goodnight.'

Emily tightened her resolve another notch, clamped her eyes shut and pretended not to hear him.

His hand stroked the smooth curve of her bottom and then his body shifted towards her in one movement, the hard wall of his stomach grazing her as he settled behind her like a set of spoons in a drawer. Her breathing quickened as she felt the probe of his arousal between her thighs, and his arms closed around her, making escape, even if she'd had the will to exercise it, impossible.

Even though she kept her back to him he was still able to bring her to the pinnacle of pleasure, with gasping groans of release that reverberated throughout her body as his rocked against hers. His own sounds of ecstasy soothed her pride; at least it wasn't just she who was rendered helpless by the touch of his hands. She too had sent him to paradise, and with that thought comforting her she drifted off to sleep, still locked in his arms.

The next three weeks passed for Emily in a haze of lazy days and passion-filled nights. A kind of unspoken truce became established between them. Damien usually left for work before she got up, and when he returned in the evening she was dressed for dinner. Sometimes they ate in; on other nights they went out. She visited Rose every few days or so.

Rose wanted her to visit even more often but Emily

didn't trust herself in case she accidentally let slip something about his aunt to Damien. The effort of keeping quiet about her clandestine relationship with Rose was taxing her already stretched nerves.

She did her best to remain civil around Damien, although by the end of the third week her temper was beginning to fray. She wasn't used to so much time on her hands and her restlessness made her snap at him when he asked her what she had planned on Friday morning as he was leaving for work.

'Nothing. A big fat nothing.'

He gave her a studied look as he deftly tied his tie. 'Why don't you come in and have lunch with me today?' he suggested. 'I'll show you around the offices, introduce you to the staff.'

She lifted one shoulder half-heartedly.

'I'll think about it.'

'Call me before twelve. I'm with clients until then.'

'I'll see.'

'As you wish.' He stooped to drop a quick kiss on her pouting mouth. 'Let me know what you decide. I've got to rush. Be good.'

She humphed and rolled over on her side, pulling the sheets back over her head.

After she heard his car leave she pushed the hair out of her eyes and swung her legs out of bed. That was when it hit her like a truck coming at full force down the highway. The nausea was so sudden and so vile she only just made it to the *en suite* bathroom before gasping out the meagre contents of her stomach. She clutched at the basin, glancing at her pale features in the mirror. Another wave hit her, making her lurch over the basin once more in desperation.

After a while it eased slightly, and she washed her face and returned to the bed to lie down until the light-headedness dissipated. She lay there in increasing panic. How could her body have betrayed her like this, falling pregnant without her permission? She wanted to blame

Damien but knew it was really her own fault. She shouldn't have stopped taking the Pill in the first place. She'd just got lazy.

She dragged herself out of bed and back to the bathroom. She had to have it confirmed first—it could be a false alarm, she reassured herself vainly.

'Oh, God!' she cried at her reflection in the fogged mirror. 'What am I going to do?'

Emily stared at the dipstick in her hand, waves of panic sweeping through her at the confirmation of the pregnancy she dreaded. She'd rushed to the pharmacy and bought a double testing kit and both of the tests told her the same truth. She was having a baby—Damien's baby.

She wished she could tell somebody, somebody who would reassure her it was all going to work out, but there was no one. She thought of calling Rose but decided against it at the last minute. Her friendship with her was still developing; she didn't want to jeopardise it by burdening her with problems that were largely insurmountable.

She'd have to face it alone—she didn't have any other choice. It wasn't as if she could tell Damien, at least not yet. Perhaps she could simply disappear from his life, pretend she'd found somebody else and move on. Her heart quaked at the thought of his reaction. He liked to be the one calling the shots; that much she had learned in the few short weeks they'd been married.

Emily caught a bus to Centennial Park and walked for two hours, thinking about her dilemma. The cooling shade of the old trees calmed her enough to make her realise she had to take better care of herself from now on. No more scanty meals and irregular exercise.

She checked her watch and, seeing it was close to twelve, wondered if she should take up Damien's offer of lunch after all. She hadn't thought to bring her mobile with her, nor did she have his number on her, but she knew where his office block was and decided to go there in person.

She wasn't sure what made her stop at the flashing pedestrian signal across the street from his building. Normally she would have raced across, just like everyone else, weaving her way through the bustling crowd, but this time she didn't.

She saw Damien first. He was outside the front entrance, bending down to speak through a car window to someone sitting in the driver's seat of a sports car. Several horns tooted behind the shiny Mercedes and Emily watched in horror as Linda Janssen leaned out of the window to kiss him, her hand grasping his, holding it to the ridge of the car's open window. A cab driver tailgated Linda's car and Damien stepped back and waved her off with a warm smile.

Emily turned and sped in the opposite direction, her heart thumping painfully in her chest. She almost fell to her knees in her haste to get away before Damien looked across the street. She checked over her shoulder once and was relieved when a line of buses blocked the intersection, giving her a lengthy reprieve.

She stumbled on to the first bus that sidled to a stop beside her, not caring where it was going. She paid her fare and huddled in a seat next to an old gentleman who smelt of mothballs and whisky. She sat and willed herself not to be sick, all the time wondering how she was going to face Damien later that day.

The bus took her to Waringah Mall, where she spent the afternoon wandering aimlessly around the shops, filling in time with cups of tea or glasses of juice from the various cafés. She was sitting staring at the uneaten raisin toast in front of her when she felt a shadow pass over her.

'Emily!' Danny Margate pulled out the chair opposite. 'What are you doing here?'

'I...' Emily gaped at him in shock. 'I'm...I'm shopping.'

Danny looked at the floor near her feet, noting the absence of any parcels.

'Not very successfully, I'd say.'

'I'm not in the mood for buying today.'

'How's Damien? Keeping you busy?'

Emily didn't care for his insolent tone. 'He's fine.'

'You don't seem very happy to see me,' he observed. 'Especially when I have something in my possession I'm sure you'll want very badly.'

She watched him closely, trying to gauge his mood. 'What is it?'

'It's a diary,' he said, picking up a slice of her abandoned raisin toast and biting into it.

'Whose?'

He paused for effect. Emily felt like a trout being lured by a colourful but totally fake fly.

'Rose's.'

She stared at him incredulously. 'You'd give me *Rose's* diary?'

His smile didn't quite reach his cold light-blue eyes. 'For a price.'

'Of course,' she said cynically.

'If you don't want it I can offer it to someone else. I already have someone in mind.'

'Who?'

'Marsha Montford.'

Emily was familiar with the biographer's work. Her last book had caused an even bigger scandal than her own. She felt sick at the thought of Damien and his aunt being subjected to the sort of ruthless tactics someone like Marsha employed to write a bestseller.

'How much?' she asked.

'How much can you afford?'

Emily took her time replying. She didn't want to commit herself, but neither did she want to give him free rein to destroy his brother and aunt in so despicable a fashion.

'I'll have to think about it,' she hedged. 'I'll call you on Monday.'

His eyes glinted with triumph. 'I'll look forward to it.' He got to his feet and handed her a business card. 'I've got a new apartment in Bondi. Come and see me there on

Monday afternoon, say two o'clock? We can finalise the terms then.'

Emily took the card, immediately feeling tainted by its presence in her hand. She felt as if she'd just stepped into a carefully laid snare, but it was too late to step back out of it now.

Danny waved a hand and was gone, disappearing into the crowd of Friday afternoon shoppers. She sat and stared at the card in her hand and wondered if today was going to get any worse. It hardly seemed likely, but she was wrong.

The bus she caught back to the city got swallowed up by a nasty traffic snarl approaching the Harbour Bridge. Emily sat clammily in the late-afternoon heat, her brow beading with perspiration in spite of the air-conditioning. The bus moved by millimetres every five minutes or so, as impatient drivers fought for their turn to merge into the already crowded lanes.

Emily began to think it would be quicker to walk, and was even considering asking the driver to open the door for her when all of a sudden the traffic started to flow. Relief seemed to spread through the bus as each of the other passengers settled back in their seats for the remainder of the journey.

She was exhausted by the time she walked up the path towards Damien's front door. A raging thirst had given her a headache and her right foot had developed a blister on the heel. It was close to seven p.m. and she knew Damien would be wondering where she was. Before she could find her key in her bag the door opened and he stood there, all six feet four of him, his dark brown eyes raking her from head to toe.

'I suppose it would be a complete waste of time to ask you where you've been?' he drawled.

She brushed past him, her right shoe in her hand. 'I could ask you the same question.'

'I was at work all day,' he said. 'Waiting for you to call.'

Emily turned to look at him. 'And was it a trying day at the office—darling?' she asked with sugar-sweet derision.

He frowned as his gaze swept over her dishevelled form. 'You don't seem to be in a very good mood,' he observed. 'Has something happened?'

She could have screamed at him. *Yes, I'm having your child!* She could hear the words forming in her throat and hastily swallowed them. This was definitely not the right time to drop that particular bombshell.

'I'm hot and tired. My bus was caught in traffic and I had to sit for an hour and twenty minutes while the lanes cleared. I have a headache too,' she added despondently. *And I saw you with your mistress in the middle of town and your brother is a creep who'd sell his grandmother to make a dollar.*

'Why don't you have a shower and I'll bring you up some paracetamol?'

Emily sighed gratefully and carried on up the stairs.

She was towelling her hair dry after her shower when he came into the *en suite* bathroom with a glass of water and two white tablets. She tucked the ends of the towel across her breasts and took the glass from him. She was raising it to her mouth just as he reached down to pick up something off the floor near the vanity basin.

'What's this?' he asked.

She stared in horror at the scrunched up packet in his hand. It was the pregnancy test she'd used that morning.

CHAPTER TWELVE

EMILY froze.

Damien unfolded the packet and stood looking at it for a long time. He scrunched it back up and tossed it in the bin near the basin. His expression when he turned to look at her was inscrutable.

'I was going to tell you—' she began uncomfortably. She cleared the restriction in her throat before continuing. 'I'm pregnant.'

'But I thought you said you were taking the Pill?' His eyes lasered hers.

Emily lowered her gaze.

'I suppose it's rather impolitic of me to ask, but is it mine?'

Her stomach churned at the contempt in his voice.

'What do you think?' she asked, hoping he'd see beyond the mask of pride in her tone.

He sucked in a breath that she felt all along the length of her spine.

'I think I'm finally starting to see why you married me.'

She didn't trust herself to speak. His eyes hardened as they bored into hers.

'I didn't just solve your financial problems, did I? I also provided a convenient safety net for your love-child. Does Danny know?'

She shook her head, close to tears at his ready assumption that this baby wasn't his. Did he really think so badly of her? That she'd use him in such a way?

He gave her a scornful look when she didn't speak.

'I can't believe you managed to pull it off. Here I was,

thinking I had outmanoeuvred you, while all the time you had me falling neatly into a snare of your own.'

'Damien, I never intended this to—'

He dismissed her with a carelessly flung hand. 'Me, of all people. The irony, if only you knew, is unbelievable.'

'It's not what you're thinking—'

'Don't try and weasel your way out of this,' he barked. 'I should've seen it coming but I didn't. Quite frankly, I didn't think you'd go so low, but then it proves how deluded us men really are. I should've known there'd be a high price to pay for the pleasure I've had from that delectable body of yours.' He gave her another sweeping glance that chilled her to the bone. 'When is it due?'

Emily was beyond the maths in her upset state. 'I'm...I'm not sure. I don't know how far along I am.'

He turned around and slammed his fist into the wall near the door. She shrank from the violence in his action, her eyes widening in alarm. She'd never seen him so out of control before and it frightened her.

'Please, Damien,' she choked. 'Please listen to me.'

He pushed himself away from the wall and faced her, his eyes like savage pools of hatred. 'I need to be on my own for a while,' he said. 'Don't wait up.'

Emily watched him leave the bathroom, her heart breaking with each step he took away from her.

She heard the front door slam and then the roar of his Lamborghini as he sped out of the driveway as if the hounds of hell were after him. She sank to the floor and bent her head into her knees. There was nothing she could do—he'd already made up his mind. There was simply nothing she could do.

Emily crawled into bed some time later and slept fitfully until she heard the sound of Damien's car returning. She heard him clatter about in the kitchen downstairs and then in the lounge, where she heard him switch on the television. The noise of the replay of a one-day cricket match made it impossible for her to go back to sleep. She listened to the background drone for a few minutes before she dragged herself out of the bed. She reached for her bathrobe and, giving the lounge a wide berth, headed for the kitchen for something to settle her squeamish stomach.

She was peering into the refrigerator when Damien spoke from behind her. 'Can I get you something? Some toast or an egg?' There was no trace of the earlier anger in his voice.

Emily shut the fridge and looked up at him. There were lines of tension around his firm mouth, but his expression remained impassive.

'I'll have some toast.' She moved towards the toaster.

'I'll get it,' he said, crossing the room. 'You sit down.'

Emily sat down on the nearest kitchen stool and watched as he took bread from the freezer compartment and popped it into the toaster.

He leant back against the bench while he waited for it to cook, his arms folded across his chest. 'I should apologise for my behaviour earlier,' he said.

'It doesn't matter.' She looked away, frightened she might start crying.

'Yes, it does.' She heard him reach for a plate and a knife. 'I hadn't taken into account at that stage the impact of this on you.'

'What do you mean?'

He turned at the pop of the toaster and began spreading the toast with the margarine he'd taken from the fridge.

'I was thinking of how your news impacted on me. I'm afraid I hadn't given much thought to how it impacted on you.'

Emily retreated into one of her helpless silences.

'I assume this pregnancy wasn't planned?'

She shook her head.

'Then what do you plan to do?'

'I...I hadn't thought that far.'

'You not intending to...' he paused as he searched for the right euphemism '...get rid of it?'

'Of course not!' She snatched at the toast he handed her and turned away. 'This is my fault—I'm the one who has to face the consequences, not the totally innocent party.'

'I don't think you should tell Danny, at least not now. I don't think he'd take it too well.'

Emily toyed with the toast on her plate with agitated fingers. Damien handed her the honey jar and a knife. Their fingers touched briefly and she pulled her hand away as if it had been burnt.

'I hate to destroy any image you might have of your expected child's father, but Danny's prime motivation in life is to make money at someone else's expense.'

'Danny isn't—'

'I know what you're going to say,' he interrupted her. 'I've heard it all before from the various girlfriends he's had in the past. I've had to pay off quite a few before you came along.'

Emily's stomach hollowed.

'I wasn't really his—'

'Quite frankly, I'm not too interested in the details.' He cut across her denial. 'Danny is somewhat of a law unto himself. You'd be wise to give him a wide berth. Why not pass this child off as mine? No one will question it.'

No one but you! she thought despairingly.

'But—'

He stalled her protest with a raised hand.

'No, I insist. It will do me good to bring up someone else's child. It will help me get a perspective on some old issues that keep cropping up.'

Emily pushed away her toast. 'Damien, I need to explain—'

'Please.' He grasped her hand, stalling her confession. 'I insist. We're both adults. We can deal with this.'

'But you don't understand!' she cried.

'Oh, but I do,' he said. 'More than you'll ever know.'

She gave up at that point. Her head was still pounding and the toast he'd made was lying untouched in front of her.

'I'm so tired,' she said in defeat.

'Come on.' He took her by the arm, helping her to her feet. 'Let's get you into bed where you belong.'

Emily leant on him gratefully, too exhausted to say the things she needed to say. Her mind was scrambled with a host of erratic thoughts. How could she prove this was Damien's child? Would he consent to a DNA test? What would he say when he finally found out the truth, or would it be too late? Hadn't they already said and done too much?

She slipped in between the cool sheets and closed her eyes. Damien drew the covers over her and stood by the bedside for a moment, thinking.

'We should call a doctor,' he said after a moment or two. 'Have you checked out.'

'I'm fine, really.'

'You don't eat properly,' he said. 'You've lost even more weight since we've been married. You've got to think about the baby.'

'I know,' she said into the pillow. 'I'll try.'

She sighed and closed her eyes, her body insisting on sleep even though her mind was tortured with the anguish of her situation. Her body won. Within minutes she was asleep, oblivious to the dark, concerned gaze of her husband, who was standing looking down at her.

The nausea hit her hard the next morning. As she dry-retched over the basin she was aware of Damien listening on the other side of the *en suite* bathroom door.

'Open the door, Emily,' he commanded.

She retched again and turned on the tap.

'I...I won't be long,' she gasped.

'Open the damn door!'

She grabbed a towel with one hand and unsnibbed the door with the other.

'Am I to be allowed no privacy?' she flared at him. 'I don't need an audience right now.'

He stepped into the bathroom, his height and breadth instantly shrinking the room. 'You shouldn't lock yourself in here. You could faint, or something, and injure yourself.'

'And why should you care?' she sniped at him. 'All your problems would be over then, wouldn't they?'

His mouth set into a tight line as he looked down at her pale features, taking in her shadowed eyes and trembling bottom lip, which she was trying to disguise by biting down on it with her straight white teeth.

'Emily...' He touched her on the shoulder but she flinched away.

'Excuse me...' She bent over the basin again and he winced at the wretched sounds of her being sick.

'Oh, Emily.' His hand on the curve of her back was gentle as he stroked her.

'I'll be...I'll be fine in a minute.'

She rinsed her mouth and washed her face. He handed her a towel and she buried her face in it.

'Perhaps I should take you to a doctor.'

'No.' She put the towel in the washing hamper. 'I just need some dry toast or something. It'll pass in a few minutes.'

'Go back to bed and I'll bring some up,' he offered.

Emily went back to the bed and lay down to wait for his return. She felt a rush of warmth at his gentle handling of her, as if he cared for her in some small way. But then, she reminded herself, he was just doing what any normal person would do for someone who was suffering.

Damien came back with tea and toast on a tray and set it down across her knees. 'Here you go—breakfast in bed.'

'Thank you.' She tentatively nibbled at a piece of wholewheat toast, conscious of his watchful gaze.

'I thought we might go out somewhere today,' he said, sitting on the edge of the bed. 'That is, if you're feeling better.'

Emily swallowed the mouthful of toast and asked, 'Where were you thinking of going?'

'What about lunch at one of the Bondi Beach cafés, followed by a leisurely walk around to Bronte? We could take our bathers and have a swim. It would do you good to get some fresh air.'

Emily wondered if Bondi was such a good idea. She didn't want to run into Danny, certainly not while she was with Damien.

'I'm not very good at beach swimming,' she prevaricated. 'I got swamped by a wave a few years ago. I only dip my toes in now.'

'I'll be with you,' he assured her. 'There's only a small swell today. I just heard the surf report on the radio.'

She knew he was making a huge effort to make peace with her and found it hard to resist his easygoing charm. It was a side of him she hadn't experienced and she wanted more of it.

'All right.' She picked up the second quarter of toast. 'I'll come.'

The crescent of Bondi Beach was a riot of colour and activity, crowds of people either sunning themselves on the golden arc of sand or swimming in the deep blue of the gently rolling swell.

They sat at one of the pavement cafés and Emily sipped at a freshly squeezed orange juice while waiting for the sandwiches Damien had ordered. An easy silence had fallen between them. Emily was trying to relax more in his company, feeling she too had to make some sort of effort as well.

'You're looking a little better already,' Damien observed as he reached for his latte.

'It's a heck of a way to start the day,' she said ruefully. 'But I've heard it only lasts a few weeks.'

'I hope so, otherwise you'll fade away to a shadow. There's not much of you now.'

'There'll soon be a whole lot more of me.' She twirled the straw in her glass reflectively.

'Emily—' He shifted in his chair slightly. 'I think we need to discuss our future.'

Emily's heart sank. She felt certain this was the part where he would inform her of his intention to release her from their marriage. The deal was off. He'd got what he wanted—the book was never going to be written now. There was no real point in continuing, especially now he was convinced she was carrying his brother's child. Was it too late to tell him the truth? All she had to do was open her mouth and say the words. But somehow she couldn't. She didn't want to tie him to her because of their child. She wanted him to love her just for her, nothing else.

She looked across at him, her fingers around the glass tightening to stop the slight tremble of her hand.

'We don't need to continue this arrangement,' he said. 'It's not appropriate under the circumstances.'

'I understand.' She lowered her eyes to the glass in her hand.

'I forced you into it, and it's not fair to expect you to carry it through.'

'When...' She cleared her throat delicately. 'When would you like me to leave?'

'What?'

She raised her eyes to his but his expression was puzzled, his brow creased in a heavy frown.

'I can go back to my apartment. Or, if the tenants don't want to vacate it just yet, I can always rent something else.'

'Emily, I'm not following you. What's this about leaving?'

Now it was her turn to look puzzled.

'Isn't that what you want?' she asked. 'For us to dissolve this marriage—or *arrangement*, as you put it.'

'I wasn't talking about ending our marriage.'

'You...you weren't?'

'No.' He shook his head. 'I was referring to our six-week deal. I'm calling it off.'

She blinked at him uncomprehendingly. 'Off?'

'Things are different now,' he said. 'You'll need support over the next few months.'

'You want me to stay?' She stared at him. 'For how long?'

He shrugged. 'For as long as it takes. It's not easy bringing up a child alone. I think we should at least make an effort to provide a stable home for him or her.'

Emily ignored the sandwiches that had arrived and focused on the tiny pearl of an orange seed in the bottom of her glass while she tried to unscramble the disorder of her brain. He wanted to stay married to her?

'Why are you doing this?' she asked, looking up again. 'After all, you accused me of setting a trap. Why should you help tie the noose about your own neck?'

He gave her a long look. 'As you said last night, why punish the only innocent party? This child has nothing to do with the machinations that brought about our marriage. And for that reason the marriage will continue in order to protect and nurture it.'

'Do I get a choice?'

'You've already made your choice. You chose to marry me, now I'm going to hold you to it.'

'By force?'

'No,' he said implacably. 'By insisting you face up to responsibility.'

'I can't see what you hope to gain by staying tied to me. Your opinion of me is hardly conducive to a happy union, especially in the long term,' she argued.

'Perhaps not, but the sex is good.'

Emily flushed and reached for a sandwich to cover her embarrassment. She bit into it and chewed slowly and purposefully so she didn't have to respond.

'I thought you'd be pleased. After all, isn't this what you planned in the first place?' he said.

'I didn't plan anything.'

He gave an embittered laugh.

'I'm finding this conversation very unpalatable,' she bit out.

'Of course you would. But it's about time we faced the implications of both our actions.'

'You're hardly innocent yourself,' she pointed out. 'Have you considered this baby might actually be yours?'

He gave her another one of the long studied looks she found so disquieting.

'The thought had crossed my mind, but I immediately dismissed it. Why else would you have consented to marrying me unless you had a desperate need to do so, and in a hurry?'

'Being a single parent these days is hardly the stigma it used to be,' she pointed out.

'But it's a whole lot easier with money behind you to back you up,' he replied with a touch of cynicism. 'And that's one thing Danny is short of right now—money.'

Emily found even the mention of Danny's name sent sparks of tension and guilt all through her, especially since their chance meeting—was it only yesterday?

'Have you seen him lately?' Damien asked unexpectedly.

'No,' she lied. 'I'm sure he's very busy with his fiancée Louise.'

'I'm afraid that's all off,' Damien announced dispassionately. 'It seems Louise got wind of the details of Danny's financial situation. He's never really been all that good with money.'

'So he comes to you for advice?'

'He comes to me for money, not advice.'

'Do you give it to him?'

'Not always,' he said, and then, changing the subject abruptly, asked, 'Are you going to contact your family about your pregnancy?'

'No.'

He gave her another of his penetrating looks. 'You're very isolationist. Is that wise?'

'I like to be independent. There's less hurt that way.'

'Who hurt you? Your parents?'

Emily scrunched up her napkin and got to her feet.

'I feel like that walk now,' she said determinedly. 'I'll wait for you outside.'

Damien watched her make her way through the knot of tables to stand watching the cool blue of the ocean in the distance. He sighed and, collecting the bill, made his way to the counter to pay for the lunch Emily had barely touched and he'd had little appetite for.

CHAPTER THIRTEEN

THEY walked in silence along the foreshore leading to Bronte Beach. Neither of them seemed inclined to speak, content to simply enjoy the view and light sea breeze that was taking the stinging heat out of the unusually warm spring day.

At one stage of the walk Damien reached for Emily's hand as she stumbled over an irregularity in the pavement. She didn't resist, but allowed his hand to swallow hers as they walked on. To others walking past them she imagined it would be easy to assume they were a devoted couple, enthusiastically planning their future together. There was no outward indication of the underlying tension simmering between them, but Emily was aching inside at the assumptions he'd made about her. It didn't seem possible to change his mind about her.

'Do you fancy a swim?' he asked as they made their way past Tamarama Bay to Bronte Beach.

Emily flicked the sticky hair out of her face and looked out across the bay. 'It's sounding more and more appealing.'

'Come on, then.' He handed her the bathers and towel he'd been carrying in his backpack. 'Go and get changed and I'll meet you here in five minutes.'

Emily made her way to the changing-rooms and slipped into her slim-fitting black bikini. She looked down at her still flat stomach and wondered how long it would be until she began to show. It didn't seem possible that inside her right now a tiny baby was beginning to grow. She thought there should be more of an outward sign, a certain glow in her features, an aura of delight clearly visible to others. But all she had was uncertainty, fear and hopelessness that the child's father thought so poorly of her.

Of course, much of it was her own fault. She'd been little less than a virago the whole time she'd been with him, fighting him at every turn. How ironic now to realise how much she loved him when there was nothing she could do to convince him of her change of heart. He'd cynically assume it was another one of her ploys to ensnare him, to get him to provide a home and security for herself and her child.

She met him outside the changing-rooms with her clothes bundled under her arm. His eyes swept over her in an appreciative male manner, lingering momentarily on the gentle curves of her breasts. He reached for her clothes and put them along with his in the backpack. Emily feasted her eyes on his long lean body, the muscles of his stomach and chest rippling as he placed her things on top of his.

'Come on.' He reached for her hand once more. 'Let's get wet.'

She followed him down to the lapping surf, her hand still in his. She hesitated once the water foamed around her ankles and he stopped and turned to her encouragingly.

'Come on, I'll hold on to you. I won't let you go.'

Emily allowed him to lead her further into the surf, wishing with all her heart that he would never let her go. She wanted to be by his side for ever, facing everything in life together—most particularly the birth of their child.

The water was now around her waist and she squealed as the cool waves lapped at her.

'That's enough,' she told him. 'I don't want to go in any deeper.'

'Where's that fighting spirit of yours?' he teased, pulling her in deeper. 'Here comes a nice wave. Turn your back and jump.'

She did as he directed and laughed when the wall of water broke over her hips, splashing her right up to her breasts.

'It's cold!' she squealed again.

'Here's another one—watch out!'

Emily turned and the wave hit her full on. She felt the rush of water drag at her legs but Damien's hand was still tightly holding hers. She brushed the hair out of her eyes and smiled up at him.

'We'll dive under the next one.' He smiled back at her. 'Once we get out a bit it's a whole lot calmer.'

'I'm not going out there!' Emily stared at the rolling breakers in front of them.

'It's just here that it's rough, where the breakers are spilling. Look out beyond that last wave—nothing, just still water.'

She clung to his hand and allowed him to lead her out. After one or two big waves caught her she realised he was not going to let her go. She suddenly found herself enjoying it. A wave would roll towards them and he'd instruct her to turn her back and jump over it, and, just like a roller coaster ride, her body would be lifted up and then put down once the wall of water had passed. It wasn't long before they were beyond the breakers, where the water was calm, the waves gently forming and rolling towards the shore, lifting their bodies from time to time before carrying on towards the sand, gathering momentum as they went.

'I've never been out this far before,' she said excitedly as she trod water beside him. 'I've always been too scared.'

Damien smiled. 'I'm glad you're starting to trust me.'

Emily waited until the next roll of water lifted them both before replying. 'But you don't trust me. That hardly seems fair, don't you think?'

He pulled her against him when a larger wave rolled towards them. Emily found her legs entwined with his, her breasts pushed up against his chest as the wave carried them forwards slightly until it went on without them to crash thunderously against the shell-encrusted shore.

He released her once the wave had gone and trod water beside her, his eyes dark and unfathomable.

'Trust is a bit like respect; you have to earn it.'

'It's very hard to earn someone's trust when they have a deep-seated bias against you,' she said, pushing a piece of floating seaweed away from her.

'You worked very hard to construct that bias, so I'm afraid you'll have to work even harder to remove it,' he said.

'So it's all up to me, then, is it?' she asked, blinking the sting of salt water out of her eyes.

'It's up to both of us. We each have to make an effort, otherwise there'd be no point in pursuing this at all.'

She wanted to tell him there *was* no point. Certainly not while he had such misunderstandings about her. But just then a larger than normal wave began building behind them and he reached for her hand once more.

'Come on, let's see if we can catch this one to the shore.'

She followed his instructions and let the wave carry her with an exhilarating rush towards the beach. The wave spat her out in the shallows and she got to her feet, her long hair like a mermaid's around her shoulders, her eyes shining with triumph.

'I did it!'

He came towards her, his tall lean body glistening in the sun, his strongly muscled thighs cutting through the swirling water like a hot knife through butter. His eyes ran over her lightly.

'So you did. Well done, and you kept your top on too. That's some achievement.'

Emily had to smile. Her bikini top was full of sand and bits of seaweed and she'd had to clutch at her bikini bottoms before she'd stood up to cover herself respectably.

'Only just.' She picked out a piece of sea lettuce from between her breasts and threw it back into the water. She looked back up at him, still smiling. 'Thanks for taking me out there. I would never have done it by myself.'

He lifted his hand and removed another piece of seaweed from her hair, his body so close to hers she could feel the warmth of his flesh. She could see the crystals of salt water clinging to his dark eyelashes. His dark hair was pushed back off his forehead, the tense lines about his mouth nowhere to be seen. She lowered her eyes to the smooth muscles of his chest, where droplets of sea water were trickling, making her ache to reach out and lick them away with her tongue...

A small child ran past them in the shallows and then toppled over as his little legs tripped in a gutter of sand underneath the foamy shallows. He came up screaming and Emily rushed to him, helping him up and reassuring him. The child's mother hurried over, carrying another small child of about a year old on one hip.

'Oh, thank you!' she said gratefully to Emily. 'He's such a tearaway at times. I only turned my back for a second and he was back in the water.'

'That's OK.' She stroked the little boy on the head. 'He's gorgeous. How old is he?'

'Three going on thirteen,' the young woman said ruefully. 'Come on, Matthew, let's go and get an ice cream.'

The little boy trotted off with his mother and baby sister, turning once to wave back at Emily.

'It seems you've got what it takes,' Damien said as they walked towards their things on the sand.

She looked up at him, hunting his face for the derision she'd come to expect. 'Meaning?'

He handed her a towel, his fingers brushing hers.

'You'll make a good mother. You have a natural affinity with children.'

She dried herself roughly as she replied, 'You say that as if you had some doubt before.'

'Not at all. I was just making an observation.'

'How comforting to know you're such an expert on determining whether a woman is good mother material or not. I'm glad I meet your exacting standards.'

He frowned at her as he slipped on his casual shirt, leaving it unbuttoned.

'Would you rather I'd said you weren't suited?' he asked gruffly. 'What is it with you? Every time I give you a compliment you throw it back in my face.'

'I'm not used to hearing compliments from you.'

'Well, then, I'll have to work on that omission. Let's start with this one: you look absolutely stunning in that almost-there black bikini. How's that?'

Emily tossed her sand-encrusted hair. 'It's a good start.'

'And I think you've got a beautiful smile when you relax enough to use it.'

She stared at him. How she wished she could tell him about her friendship with Rose. She still didn't understand why Rose insisted she keep quiet about it. It just didn't make any sense.

'But I suppose Danny's told you that many times,' he added cynically when she didn't respond.

'Danny's full of insincere compliments. I learned not to pay too much attention.'

'Wise of you.'

They continued walking along in silence, the warmth of the afternoon sun soaking into their bodies. When they got back to Bondi Beach it was even more crowded than it had been earlier.

'Let's grab a coffee before we head home,' he suggested, leading her across the busy street.

She fell into step beside him and when he finally found a vacant seat for her she slipped into it gratefully. She felt tired and more than a little out of her depth. He seemed so unreachable most of the time—aloof, distant, as if he didn't quite know what to do with her. They'd shared such intimacy, but ever since he'd found out about her pregnancy he'd kept his distance, hardly touching her, as if he couldn't bear to do so. It made her feel so empty and alone, and she craved his touch all the more, even though she knew it was hopeless. His love was directed elsewhere—to Linda Janssen. She'd seen it with her own eyes; there was no point in pretending it didn't exist. It did, and it was tearing her heart apart to even think about it.

The coffees arrived and Emily busied herself with toying with the milky froth of her latte with her teaspoon.

'Emily.'

She looked up from her coffee; his eyes were on her, his expression serious.

'Yes?'

He stirred his coffee absently before saying, 'I think it's about time I took you to visit my aunt.'

Emily's fingers on her teaspoon stilled. 'Has...has she requested it?' she asked.

He gave a rueful half-smile. 'Rose has been wanting to meet you for weeks, but I wasn't sure it was the right thing to do. I've decided it's time.'

'What you mean is you didn't think I could be trusted, isn't that more to the point?' she asked with a resentful edge to her voice.

'What I think is largely irrelevant,' he said evenly. 'Rose wants us both to come to dinner tonight.'

'Does she know...' Emily chewed her lip briefly. 'Have you told her about—?'

'No.' His eyes moved away from hers. 'I couldn't quite bring myself to do it. She'll find out soon enough. Perhaps you could announce it at dinner.'

'I'm not sure my pregnancy would be an appropriate topic for a Double Bay dinner party,' she said. 'Especially since you're claiming not to be the father.'

The silence was palpable. She lifted her eyes to his and then wished she hadn't. The hard glint of barely suppressed anger reflected there frightened her.

'How did you find out where she lives?'

Emily blinked at him, wondering what to say. He pushed his half-finished coffee away and stood up. She got to her feet and followed him out of the café, her steps dragging.

'Get in the car,' he commanded, opening the door for her, his tone frigid.

'Damien, I—'

'Get in the damn car.'

She got in the car and he shut the door heavily. She sat nervously as he went to the driver's side and got in.

'I expressly forbade you to make any contact with my aunt,' he ground out as he started the car. 'That was part of the deal.'

'I didn't make contact with your aunt,' she said. 'She made contact with me. Literally.'

Damien turned to look at her, his hands still white-knuckled on the steering wheel.

'When? What do you mean?'

'When you were interstate. I walked into her in the street three doors from your house and nearly knocked her over.'

He turned back to the task of driving through the intersection, his mouth set into a grim line. 'What a windfall that must have been,' he derided. 'Tell me, did you take notes?'

'Of course not! It was nothing like that.'

'I don't believe you.'

'So, what else is new?' she chipped at him. 'You don't believe a lot of things I tell you. Why should this be any different?'

'How many times have you seen her?'

'Several.'

He drove on in a rigid silence. Emily sat with her head turned to the passing scenery, her eyes seeing nothing. After a long pause he turned to glance at her.

'Why didn't you tell me?'

'Because she told me not to.'

The traffic moved ahead and he turned back to concentrate on his driving.

'All the same, you should have told me.'

'What? And break a confidence?' She glared across at him. 'You're always telling me how untrustworthy I am, how I'd do anything for a good story. I decided to prove you wrong for once.'

He frowned as he took the turn to Double Bay.

'I don't understand why she'd do that. She insisted I stop your book at all costs.'

'Marrying me was rather an extreme measure, don't you think?'

'It was all I could think of at the time,' he said drily, turning into his driveway.

'What a pity you didn't have time to think of something more dastardly, like boiling me in oil or tying me up for the crows to pick at.'

'Believe me—' he glanced at her darkly as he stopped the engine '—I haven't ruled those things out.'

She tossed her head as she got out of the car.

'I wouldn't advise it,' she warned. 'Your aunt likes me, and I like her.'

'Female solidarity,' he muttered. 'I never would've guessed.'

She followed him into the house, determined not to be intimidated by his mood. Why should she be the one feeling guilty when she'd done nothing wrong? Rose Margate had approached her, and once she'd felt comfortable with her had asked to continue the acquaintance. Emily hadn't engineered any part of it, nor had she wanted to keep the arrangement quiet, as Rose had insisted.

Emily headed for the shower, leaving Damien to bring in the wet and sandy towels. Her head ached from the tension of it all, her skin felt the sting of a little too much sun and her heart felt heavy with its burden of love for a man who always believed the worst of her.

When she came downstairs an hour later he was talking on the telephone in the lounge. His gaze swept over her, taking in the close-fitting white sundress that offset the golden glow of her sun-kissed skin. Her strappy red sandals and simple red purse tied in beautifully with the colourful scarf she had used to draw her hair back from her face. The red-rose lipstick and dark mascara she wore were her only make-up apart from a spray of her favourite perfume.

He finished the call and faced her, his expression full of self-reproach. 'It seems I have an apology to make.'

'Oh?' Her tone was flippant. 'Let me guess—your aunt Rose verified my story, so now it's OK to believe me?'

His mouth tightened. 'Look, my aunt has refused to see anyone other than her driver, her doctor and me for years. You can hardly blame me for being suspicious.'

'Would you like to check my purse before we go tonight?' She handed it to him. 'Just in case I've slipped in my Dictaphone or a miniature camera.'

He ignored her outstretched purse and looked at her grimly.

'I don't wish to argue with you. The very fact that Rose has invited anyone to her house this evening is a miracle. Let's not spoil it for her by sniping at each other.'

'Fine by me.' She tossed her head.

They walked in silence towards Rose's house. Emily glanced at Damien once or twice but decided against making idle conversation. She could tell by the set of his jaw he was keeping himself under some sort of iron control, as if he didn't trust himself not to tell her what he really thought of her.

He finally broke the long silence as he opened Rose's front gate.

'I understand my aunt has informed you of her condition?'

'Yes.'

'I assume you understand how important it is to her that this goes no further than you or me?'

'Does Danny know?' she asked.

His glance towards her was razor-sharp.

'Not that I'm aware of. And unless Rose insists otherwise it'd better stay that way.'

Emily didn't like the way he was looking at her, as if she were the one most likely to spill the beans.

'He won't hear it from me,' she assured him.

'Good.'

* * *

Rose was dressed in a long flowing gown that looked as if it had previously been one of her theatre costumes. Emily loved the way she carried it off, in a manner that bordered on the eccentric. She waved a glass of soda water in one hand just like a fan and Emily watched as she swept Damien into her arms, just as a mother would a long-lost son. The obvious affection between Rose and Damien brought a lump to the back of Emily's throat as she waited her turn to greet her.

'Emily, you look ravishing—doesn't she, Damien?' Rose kissed both her cheeks and smiled broadly at her. 'Was he very cross at our little secret, my dear?' she added, winking towards the tall figure of her nephew standing at her shoulder.

Emily flicked a glance towards him as she answered, 'He took it very well, all things considered.'

Damien's eyes glinted, but she averted her gaze and, turning her attention to Rose's dress, asked, 'Is that one of your stage costumes?'

'Yes, *The Taming Of The Shrew*. Isn't it marvellous? Such a shame to gather moths in the wardrobe. I thought I'd air it tonight, since this is such a special occasion.'

'It is?' Emily looked between Rose and Damien as if she'd missed out on some important bit of information.

'Yes,' said Rose. 'I've invited someone else this evening. Someone very special to Damien and me.'

Emily glanced back at Damien but his expression was inscrutable.

'Who?' she asked, turning back to Rose.

Rose grinned, looking as pleased as Punch that her first social gathering in fifteen years had begun so well.

'Linda,' she said proudly. 'Linda Janssen.'

CHAPTER FOURTEEN

EMILY plastered a smile to her face and fought against the desire to faint.

'She'll be here soon,' Rose was saying. 'Andre can't make it unfortunately—some stomach bug or other. Now, what can I get you both to drink? Champagne?'

Emily shook her head. 'I'll just have a soda water, thank you.'

Rose's glance was speculative.

'I've got a lovely white wine if you'd prefer?'

'Emily's not much of a drinker, Aunt Rose.' Damien came to her rescue. 'I'll have some champagne, though. What sort is it?'

He distracted his aunt by investigating the expensive-looking bottle she had sitting in the ice-bucket, and Emily felt relieved beyond expression. She sat on one of the velvet sofas and tried to prepare herself for what was ahead.

What was Rose doing, inviting both her and Linda on the same evening? What did she hope to achieve? Rose knew of the gossip that surrounded Damien and Linda. Emily herself had witnessed their relationship in the middle of the city the day before. What could possibly be gained by rubbing her nose in it like this tonight? It didn't seem the sort of thing Rose would do. Perhaps she hoped to smooth things over in this polite social gathering, was doing what she thought was best for her nephew's marriage by confronting the issues head on.

Emily stared at the bubbles of soda in her glass and wished herself a thousand miles away. How had her life come to this?

The doorbell sounded and Rose left them while she went

to answer it. Emily glanced at Damien, but he was standing twirling the contents of his glass, looking out of the window, his back turned towards her.

Rose came back in raptures over Linda Janssen's long elegant mulberry outfit. Emily immediately felt gauche in her simple white sundress and got to her feet, her expression guarded.

'Damien.' Linda moved across the room and kissed both his cheeks affectionately. 'And Emily.' She turned to where Emily was standing awkwardly. 'You look lovely. Marriage suits you—every time I see you you look more beautiful.'

Emily didn't know what to say. Linda's comments gave all the appearance of sincerity, but she wondered privately what might have been said instead if Damien and his aunt weren't standing there.

'Thank you,' she managed to say. 'I hope your husband is feeling better soon.'

Linda waved a dismissive hand as she accepted the glass of champagne Damien handed her.

'He's fine. Just a stomach thing. Now, tell me, Rose, what is this all about? It's been positively years since you've had guests. What brought about this totally unexpected event?'

Rose sat down on the edge of one of the sofas, her face radiant.

'I have something I wish to announce.'

Emily sat on the edge of her seat, wondering if Damien had told his aunt of her pregnancy.

'What is it?' Linda, too, was on the edge of her seat.

Rose paused. It was obvious to Emily that something of great importance was about to be announced.

'I'm going to have an operation,' Rose said at last.

'An operation?' Linda and Damien spoke in unison.

'What sort of operation?' Emily put in.

'A life-changing one,' Rose announced proudly. 'I'm going to have an experimental operation to implant stem cells into part of my brain. The part that is causing the Parkinson's Disease.'

There was an awed silence.

'Well?' Rose got to her feet. 'Aren't you going to say anything?'

Damien got to his feet first and hugged his aunt. 'Are you sure it's safe? Have you considered the possibility of it going wrong? What then?'

'Damien, darling—' Rose touched his hand with her trembling one '—I can't live like this any more. Shut away here like a hermit, hiding from the public in case they think I'm drunk. I have to do this—it's my only chance.'

'What are the risks?' Linda asked.

Rose turned to face her. 'Of course there are risks, but I have to take them. Epilepsy, paralysis, permanent brain damage.'

'Oh, no!' Emily gasped.

Rose turned to her and laid a hand on her shoulder reassuringly. 'Don't worry, my dear. I've considered all the risks and compared to what I'm already suffering I don't think I have much to lose. I don't want to live like this any more. And in some ways you've been responsible for my decision.'

'I...I have?' Emily stared at her.

'Yes. You've forced me to realise I can't expect the public to simply accept my disappearance. They want answers. I owe that to them.'

'You don't owe them anything,' Damien said implacably.

Rose swivelled to look at her nephew. 'Damien, darling, Emily is right. I wouldn't have the things I have if it hadn't been for my public. I've been well supported over the years. It's time I faced reality. I can't expect the public to be fobbed off with vague excuses any longer. I want the truth to be told.'

'But Aunt Rose—!' Damien protested.

'No.' She held up her hand in protest. 'I've made up my

mind. I'm going ahead with this operation and I'm determined it will be a success. A positive attitude is what I need. Who knows? I might even perform again.'

'Are you serious?' Linda asked. 'But that would be marvellous! A miracle, in fact.'

'I know,' Rose said, 'and if I do I'd like Emily to write about my comeback.'

'Aren't we jumping the gun a bit, here?' Damien interrupted. 'You haven't had the surgery yet. It's probably a bit early to be planning Emily's book signing.'

Emily glared at him resentfully.

'Oh, darling.' Rose smiled at him fondly. 'I realise you're trying to protect Emily from further disappointment, but think about it. If I do make a good recovery it will make up for giving up her book. I feel I owe that to her at least.'

'You don't owe me anything, Rose,' Emily said quietly.

'Oh, but I do.' Rose was insistent.

'When is the surgery to take place?' Damien asked.

'At the end of next week,' Rose said. 'Of course, this operation is still in the experimental stages, but some success has already been achieved and my doctor thinks it's worth a try.'

'I think you're very brave,' Emily said.

'What about the press?' Damien asked. 'How are we to keep this private? Doctors and nurses are meant to maintain a confidential silence, but what about the other ward staff? One whiff of your name and someone stands to make a fortune out of it.'

Emily didn't know where to look. Damien's comments seemed to be directed towards her, as if he didn't trust her not to rush out and release a press statement immediately.

'Of course I'd like to keep things quiet for as long as possible,' Rose said. 'But it's a large teaching hospital and this procedure will attract a lot of attention. I'm prepared for that.' She looked at Damien directly, her dark eyes, so like his, bright with courage and conviction. 'I must do this, Damien. It's my last chance. Surely you must see that?'

Damien sighed and, putting down his drink, gave his aunt another warm hug. 'I see that you're a very determined woman who wants another grab at centre stage.'

'And why shouldn't I?' Rose smiled up at him when he released her. 'With you married now I feel I've got something to live for. God willing, there'll be great-nephews and nieces, and I want to be in good health to enjoy them.'

'Don't rush the poor darlings, Rose.' Linda laughed. 'They've only been married a few weeks.'

Emily wanted the sofa to open up and swallow her. She felt the heat of Damien's gaze on her but resolutely kept her eyes averted. She didn't know what to make of Linda. She seemed to be very fond of Rose, and didn't appear to be uncomfortable at all at being in the same room as Damien's new wife. Was she so brazen, and he so without shame, that they would openly flaunt their clandestine relationship in such a way? There was certainly an intimacy about them both. Emily could see it in the way they looked at each other occasionally. A little smile, a knowing glance, the comfort and ease with which they greeted each other, usually with a kiss to both cheeks or a gentle squeeze of the hand.

Emily sipped at her drink and tried to stop looking at them. It was like a form of torture and she couldn't imagine why Rose encouraged it.

The conversation moved to other things, and soon after Rose directed them to the elegantly laid table in the dining room.

'Of course, I'm not much of a cook,' she confessed. 'I organised for Charlie to pick me up some take-away earlier.'

'And not just any old take-away.' Linda smiled knowingly at Damien and Emily's heart gave another tight squeeze of pain. 'Knowing Rose, it will be no less than some five-star restaurant she's found in the telephone book.'

Damien grinned and poured Emily another glass of soda water while they waited for Rose to bring in the first course.

'Should I help her?' Emily half rose in her chair but Damien's hand settled on hers, stalling her.

'No, sit down. She hasn't played hostess for years. Let her have her fun.'

Emily sat back down and wished she could think of something to say to contribute to the lively conversation Linda was having with Damien, but her mind kept wandering, going off at useless tangents to where her heart wasn't breaking and her dreams weren't being smashed by the hard heels of reality.

'What do you think, Emily?' Linda asked some time later, looking at her intently.

'Sorry?' Emily blinked, dragging her attention back. 'Did you say something?'

Linda smiled patiently. 'I asked if you thought Danny should be told about Rose's surgery?'

Emily looked at Damien, but his expression was closed.

'He...well, he is her nephew too,' she said cautiously. 'But isn't that up to Rose?'

'What's up to me?' Rose came in at that point, balancing a tray of oysters topped with sour cream and caviare.

'We were discussing whether or not you wanted Danny to know about your operation,' Linda said.

Rose handed round the entrées and waited until she'd sat down before replying.

'I'd like to keep Danny out of this, if you don't mind. I realise blood is thicker than water and all that, but Danny has rather a tainted sense of family loyalty, don't you agree?'

Emily bent her head to her oysters and hoped her face wasn't as hot and flushed as it felt. The very mention of Danny's name caused her to feel guilt-stricken, and with Damien sitting beside her, and his opinion on the paternity of the child she was carrying, she knew it only made her reaction all the more damning.

'Danny has quite a lot of responsibilities he has yet to accept,' Damien said after a slight pause. 'And I, for one, am going to make certain he faces up to them.'

'Don't tell me he's got another girl into trouble?' Rose asked, reaching for her wine. 'After that last one I would've thought he'd have learnt his lesson.'

Emily was sure she was going to be sick. The oysters on her plate seemed to be staring at her, taunting her with their grotesque little deformed shapes, the caviare swirling into a red globule that looked just like blood.

'Excuse me...' She pushed herself from the table, stumbling over the edge of Damien's chair.

'Emily! Are you all right?' Rose and Linda spoke in concerned unison.

Damien was on his feet, and his hand came around her so quickly that Emily didn't have time to fall. She pushed out of his hold to get to the bathroom, her face as white as a sheet. She could hear Linda's sympathetic tones trailing after her as she left.

'Andre was the same. Sick as a dog. It's this wretched bug that's going around. Poor Emily.'

Emily heaved into Rose's pink shell-like basin, too far gone to care that Damien was at her shoulder, witnessing her distress.

He handed her a face cloth, his other arm stroking the clammy skin under the back of her hair.

'I shouldn't have made you come out tonight,' he said. 'You really needed a quiet night at home.'

Emily washed her face and steadied herself against the basin.

'Yes, well, given a choice I would've preferred my own company to that of your mistress, charming as she is.'

Damien met her shadowed eyes in the mirror.

'Emily, there's something you need to know about Linda,' he began awkwardly.

Emily turned and faced him, their bodies so close they were almost touching. Damien stepped back to give her more room.

'You love her, don't you?' she said in a flat tone.

Damien's eyes gave nothing away.

'I saw you,' she continued bitterly before he could respond. 'In town yesterday. I was coming to have lunch with you. You were outside your office; quite touching it was. She was blocking the traffic and you were leaning down to talk to her. Probably telling her your wife doesn't understand you and asking could you meet her later.'

'Emily—' He frowned heavily. 'You don't understand. It's not—'

'I don't understand?' she flared at him, uncaring that their voices were probably carrying. 'You know what I don't understand? I don't understand why I'm part of all this.' She waved her hand around to encompass their surroundings. 'I planned to write a book—against my better judgement, I might add, but I was desperate to make ends meet. Suddenly I find myself married to one of the key characters, who happens to be embroiled in an affair with one of his partner's wives. I find myself becoming overly attached to the subject of my book, who then decides to come out of hiding after years of seclusion. I'm forced to sit through an evening with your mistress casting loving looks your way across the table, and on top of that I'm expected to eat oysters as if nothing is wrong.'

'I realise how difficult this has been for you—'

'Difficult?' she railed at him. 'You have no idea of what this is like for me.'

'I understand, believe me. As soon as Danny's name was mentioned I knew you'd find it awkward. But the sooner you get used to the idea that Danny is not going to stand by you, the better. He's just not capable of it.'

'This is not about Danny!' she cried. 'This is about you and me.'

'I've already told you I'll accept the child as mine,' he said, lowering his voice. 'No one need know other than us.'

Emily turned back to the basin, her hands clenched as if hanging on to a lifeline.

'Damien.' Her tone was bleak. 'I need to tell you something. Something important.'

'No,' he said. 'I need to tell you something first. It's about Linda.'

Emily turned back to face him, her eyes widening in panic. He wanted to leave her for Linda; she was sure of it.

'Linda is—'

'Emily? Are you all right?' Rose's voice was just outside the door. 'Damien? Shall I call the doctor?'

Damien sighed and, leaving Emily to wash her face, opened the bathroom door to his aunt.

'That won't be necessary, Aunt Rose,' he said reassuringly. 'We spent the day at the beach. Emily's had a little too much sun. I'll take her home shortly.'

His aunt murmured something Emily didn't catch as she rinsed her face one more.

He turned back to her once his aunt had gone. 'Do you want me to take you home?'

Emily shook her head. 'This is your aunt's first dinner party in fifteen years or so. I don't want to be the one to spoil it.'

'I don't mind,' he said. 'I can always come back once I've taken you home.'

Yes, Emily thought. *And continue where you left off with Linda Janssen.*

'Do what you like,' she said defeatedly. 'It's all the same to me.'

Damien sighed. 'Come on,' he said heavily. 'I'll take you home.'

He helped her into the house and hovered around as she made preparations for going to bed.

'Shouldn't you have something to eat?' he asked as she pulled the bed covers back.

'I'm not hungry.'

'That seems to be your stock phrase,' he commented drily. 'But it's hardly one that will ensure the health and well-being of your expected infant.'

'I can't see that it can be any concern of yours,' she said, brushing past him to reach for her wrap.

'Someone has to be concerned,' he said.

'Don't trouble yourself.' She tied the ends of her wrap viciously. 'Anyway, I find your hypocrisy nauseating.'

'And my presence as well, I take it?'

She flashed him a malevolent glance. 'Go figure.'

He turned and left her without another word. Emily stared at the empty space he'd so recently occupied and bit her lip. She didn't like herself in this mood, but what did he expect? How could he expect her to tolerate an evening in the company of his latest fling and not complain?

She threw herself across the huge bed and sobbed until there were very few tears left. She felt exhausted. Physically and mentally drained. As if all her energy had been tapped.

She must have slept. She woke to the sounds of someone moving about the house downstairs and sat up, brushing the hair out of her face and listening intently.

She heard Damien's tread on the stairs. She'd become aware of every sound he made, her senses on full alert to his every move. He opened the bedroom door but she didn't have time to slip down beneath the covers again and pretend to be asleep.

'How are you feeling?' he asked, turning on the lamp by the bedside.

'I'm hungry,' she said honestly, blinking at the increase in light.

'I'll get you something,' he offered. 'Aunt Rose sent a doggy bag for you in case you were feeling better.'

'Not oysters, I hope?'

He gave a wry half-smile. 'No, not oysters.'

He came back with a dainty portion of lemon chicken with spinach-flecked wild rice and a shell-like bread roll, all laid out on a tray, complete with damask napkin and silver cutlery.

Emily picked up her fork and nibbled at the food, conscious of his silent watchful gaze.

'I hope Rose wasn't too disappointed about me leaving,' she said between mouthfuls.

'She wasn't disappointed, just concerned.' He sat on the end of the bed and undid his black shoes. 'I had to promise I wouldn't upset you. She was most insistent.'

'And did you promise?'

He swung his legs around to face her. She could see the tired lines etched in his face, his broad shoulders slightly slumped. He undid his tie and tossed it carelessly to the wing chair in the corner.

'It has never been my intention to upset you,' he said wearily. He lay down across the end of the bed, one of his shoulders just near her feet. He put one arm over his eyes, as if the light from the shielded globe above him was too bright for his tired eyes. 'But I seem to have got us both into a God-awful mess, all the same.'

Emily wasn't sure what to say. Her appetite had waned and she crumbled the bread roll with restless fingers as she sat there watching him.

'The truth is, you caught me off-guard,' he said.

'I...I did?'

He still lay with his eyes closed against the light.

'Your interest in Rose was too close for comfort. I had to do something to stop you writing about her. Marrying you was taking it to extremes, I know, but I didn't really stop to think. I had to protect Rose and Linda, no matter what.'

'Linda?' Emily straightened in agitation at the mention of that name. 'Why protect Linda? What has she got to do with Rose?'

Damien levered himself up off the bed, his gaze meshing with her questioning one.

'Because,' he said slowly and deliberately, 'Linda is Rose's illegitimate daughter.'

CHAPTER FIFTEEN

'LINDA'S your *cousin*?' Emily stared at him, her mouth dropping open. 'You're having an affair with *your cousin*?'

Damien shook his head, giving her a world-weary look.

'I've said this so many times I'm sick of saying it. Linda Janssen and I are not having, have never had, nor will ever have an affair. However, I do care for her, very deeply. Both she and Rose have suffered greatly in the years they've been apart and I promised myself I'd do anything I could to protect them from any further pain, as you've more or less gathered.'

Emily pushed the tray to one side with unsteady hands.

'Does...does Danny know?'

'I think he suspects something, but so far we've been able to keep him out of it. Linda and Rose have only recently been reunited. Rose told me tonight she's been wanting to tell you for weeks but Linda had sworn her to secrecy. She didn't want the press to get wind of it and blow it all up in their faces. Linda's adoptive parents needed time to adjust to their daughter activating the search for her mother. It was fraught with legal difficulties, and then you came in, informing the public of your plans to release a biography on Rose. It was a potential minefield and I had to act quickly.'

Emily needed time to absorb his words. They'd impacted on her deeply. She didn't know how to deal with the fact that she'd been so wrong about him; that she'd been so blind. She'd accused him of having an affair when all the time he'd been trying to protect the two people he loved deeply. She'd planned to write about the family as if they were characters in a play of her own devising, not real people at all, with real emotions, real pain. She felt so ashamed.

She knew her silence was condemning her, but she couldn't engage her mind and mouth to say the words she needed to say. To ask for the forgiveness she silently craved, to tell him of her own doubts and fears that had driven her from her unhappy childhood headlong into the deep, dark, secretive pool of his, stirring up secrets and adding to the speculation that had dogged him most.

'I'll leave you to get some rest.' He spoke across her jumbled thoughts. 'I'm flying to Brisbane tomorrow with Linda. I'm going to meet her adoptive parents, encourage them to meet Rose. They've resisted so far, but Linda feels it might help if I talk to them.'

'Because of your own experiences?' she managed to ask.

He gave her a long studied look.

'Rose told you, didn't she?'

Emily nodded, unable to speak, emotion clogging her throat, but he'd already turned away and didn't see the glitter of tears welling in her eyes.

'I want Linda to have what I missed out on. A proper and loving relationship with her natural mother.'

'I understand,' she said once she had control of her voice, but when she looked up he'd already gone.

When Monday finally came around, after one of the longest Sundays in Emily's life, she changed her mind about visiting Danny at the address he'd given her. Instead, she called him on his mobile and left a message for him to meet her at Damien's house. She felt safer that way, not trusting him to fulfil his side of the deal.

Emily looked at her watch. She had five minutes. Everything she owned was contained in the single bank cheque that lay in between the pages of her appointment diary on the sideboard. She'd sold her apartment within hours of releasing it. The real estate agent had at first questioned her haste, but he'd had an anxious buyer in the wings and the deal had been signed and with the lawyers before lunchtime.

She checked her watch. Three minutes.

She opened the door on his second knock and felt instantly nauseated as his greedy eyes ran over her.

'I'm on time, Emily,' he said suavely.

'Let's get this over with.' Her tone was dark. 'Where's the diary?'

His cold blue eyes chilled her to the marrow but she held his gaze.

'Where's the money?' he asked.

'We never did discuss how much you want.'

'You know me, Em.' His eyes ran over her. 'I've got expensive tastes.'

'I can't—won't negotiate on this,' she said. 'Like you, I have limited funds.'

His lip curled. 'Isn't my brother paying his way?'

Her eyes glittered with anger. 'I can't imagine what you mean by that.'

'Can't you?' He laughed.

'No.'

'Hasn't he bribed his way into your bed yet?'

She knew she was blushing but could do nothing to stop it. 'He didn't have to resort to such tactics,' she said. 'I went quite willingly.'

His eyebrows rose speculatively. 'Yet again he seems to have succeeded where I failed.'

'You're insanely jealous of him, aren't you?' she asked.

'Jealous?' His icy eyes spat chips at her. 'He's got nothing I want.'

'No, I imagine not. Common decency and loyalty aren't qualities highly valued in your book. You'd rather sell your soul than protect those who have loved and supported you.'

'I suppose you're referring to my aunt Rose?' His mouth curled again. 'She never had eyes for anyone but Damien. I didn't get a look in.'

'At least you had two parents who loved you.'

'All the love in the world doesn't pay the bills. I need money to survive, and Aunt Rose is hardly likely to leave me anything with Damien standing in the way.'

Emily frowned in disbelief at his callousness.

'This is all about money, isn't it?' she asked. 'You don't care about your aunt or Damien, do you? You can't possibly care about your family, otherwise I wouldn't be standing here offering you money for a diary no one has any business seeing.'

'But you want it, don't you, sweet Emily?' he sneered at her. 'You want it so bad. You can finally find out all of Rose's secrets and make your million dollars in royalties.'

She looked at him in disgust. 'Of course I want the diary, but not for the reasons you think.'

'I don't care why you want it, you stuck-up little bitch. Just give me what you've got and I'll go.'

'Not until I tell you what I think of you,' she flashed at him angrily. 'You used me to get back at your family and I can never forgive you for that.'

'Don't make me laugh!' Danny rocked back on his heels. 'You came sniffing around me for information. I just gave you what you wanted.'

'You exploited your own flesh and blood! How can you live with yourself?'

'Don't get all hoity-toity on me, Em,' he taunted her. 'You're the one who's exploited the Margate name. Tell me, was it worth it?'

'What do you mean?' She eyeballed him suspiciously.

'Was it worth marrying my brother? I mean, you could've written the book and fought it out in court. Why did you marry him? Was it just the money?'

'No,' she said implacably. 'It was never about money.'

'Don't tell me you love him—that would really make me laugh.'

She tightened her hands together and stayed silent, not trusting herself to answer him. He looked at her closely, his hooded eyes narrowing.

'You've fallen for him, haven't you?' he asked. 'You're wasting your time,' he added when she remained silent. 'He's only got eyes for that Janssen woman. Even her husband turns a blind eye.'

He doesn't know! she reassured herself. *He doesn't know!*

'Tell me something, Danny.' She walked to the sideboard, picked up her appointment book and faced him. 'Have you read your aunt Rose's diary?'

His shoulders lifted in a shrug. 'I've skimmed it, but I knew as soon as I found it you'd be interested. Now, let's get down to business.' His tone was becoming increasingly impatient. 'Give me the money.'

'Give me the diary.' She held out her hand, her stance determined.

'The money first.'

'I want to see the diary.'

'Try before you buy, eh, Em?' He reached into the inner pocket of his loose-fitting jacket. 'Wise of you.'

He handed her a worn leather-bound pocket-sized journal. She desperately tried to disguise the tremble of her hand as she took it. She felt tainted just touching it, never mind opening it.

She handed him her cheque and his eyes widened as he looked at the figure written there.

'Not bad.' He whistled through his teeth. 'Damien must be paying dearly for the privilege of sleeping with you. What a pity I didn't actually get around to sampling you for myself.'

She didn't care for the sudden lascivious glitter in his frosty gaze as it ran over her once more.

'But then,' he added, 'as someone so wisely said, "There's no time like the present."'

He reached for her, but she'd seen it coming and stepped backwards. She tripped over the coffee table and landed awkwardly. She righted herself just in time to see Damien send Danny flying across the room with a single punch that sickened her with its intensity. She closed her eyes against the violence, her stomach churning at the thought of Damien being hurt and she being too weak and pathetic to assist him.

She shouldn't have worried. She opened her eyes to find him in front of her, offering her a hand. His dark hair was ruffled, the corner of his mouth was bleeding slightly and his right eye looked as if it was going to bruise horribly.

'He's gone,' he said, still breathing hard. 'He won't hurt you now.'

She took his hand and got to her feet, her unsteady legs threatening to let her down when she needed them most.

'I got the diary,' she said weakly, handing it to him. 'I got the diary...'

'Yes.' He took it and put it down on the coffee table. 'I know you did.'

She looked up at him for a long moment. His eyes were warm and his mouth had softened, leaving no trace of the rigid lines of tension she was used to seeing there. His hands were on her arms, holding her to him, close but not quite touching.

'Why did you marry me, Emily?' he asked.

She couldn't hold his questioning gaze.

'I...I'm not sure...' She bit her lip and, lowering her eyes, concentrated on the open neck of his shirt instead. 'I think I needed to belong to someone—anyone.'

'Anyone?'

She met his eyes bravely.

'Not just anyone—you.'

He smiled and pulled her into the shelter of his warm body.

'You have no idea how much I've longed to hear that,' he said against her hair. 'No idea at all.'

She breathed in the scent of him—a mixture of maleness and physical exertion and aftershave that sent her senses reeling.

'I have to tell you something, Damien,' she said against his chest. 'Something very important.'

He held her away from him to look down at her.

'You don't need to tell me. I already know.'

She gazed up at him questioningly.

'I heard it all,' he told her. 'I came home and saw Danny's car. I decided to come in the back door and listen for a while. I learnt some things about my brother I didn't know before, and some things about myself that shame me. Can you ever forgive me? I treated you appallingly. I have no excuse other than that I was as jealous as hell and jealousy blinded me to the truth that was staring me in the face all the time. I had so many preconceived ideas about you, but every day I spent with you showed me what a beautiful person you are. You hide behind a sharp wit and acid tongue but underneath you're vulnerable and fragile. I should've realised it the day we were married.'

'Are you...are you disappointed about the baby?' she asked cautiously. 'I didn't mean it to happen. I hadn't taken the Pill for months because...well, because I didn't need to. I didn't believe it could happen so easily. I'm so sorry. It's all my fault.'

'No.' His finger halted her speech by pressing against her soft lips. 'You are not to blame. I am. And I hereby accept full responsibility by insisting you stay married to me for the next fifty years or so.'

'You don't have to do that,' she said. 'I can—'

'You can what?' he asked. 'You've just sold your only asset. You have nothing to back you. How can you think of doing this alone?'

She bit her lip and stared at his neck again.

'Come on, Emily,' he urged. 'Tell me you need me. I need to hear it much more than you need to say it.'

She looked up at him at that.

'I love you,' she said. 'Do you know, you're the first person I've really loved since I was a child?'

He smiled and held her close, his words stirring her hair

when he spoke. 'I love you more than I can say. You're everything to me. I think that's why I acted so outrageously by insisting you marry me as I did. I didn't want anyone or anything to get in the way of my desire to tie myself to you.'

'I don't understand.' She looked up at him incredulously. 'I thought you hated me.'

'I thought I did too, but my body had other ideas. Has it convinced you enough, or should I actively engage it to convince you a bit more?'

She smiled, her eyes dancing with happiness. 'I'm not entirely convinced, but perhaps you have something in mind that will finally persuade me?'

His mouth came down and hovered just above hers.

'I thought I'd start with this.' He kissed her soundly. 'And then I thought I'd move on to this—' He kissed her again, but this time deeply, his tongue searching and finding hers. 'And then...'

She sighed as his hands sought and found her breasts.

'I'm still not quite convinced.'

His hands moved lower.

'I'm not finished yet,' he said huskily. 'But give me time.'

She smiled against his searching mouth.

'You have all the time in the world.'

Emily and Damien met Linda outside the recovery unit. Linda was pale; her hands would have been trembling except she had them so tightly clenched they didn't get a chance.

'Have you heard?' Linda asked.

'What? Is everything all right?' Damien asked, reaching for her hands.

'She's come through,' Linda said in a rush of relief. 'The doctor is pleased with her recovery so far. He said it's still too early to be sure but he thinks it went very well.'

Emily felt the sting of tears in her eyes as she saw the

comfort and support Damien was giving to his cousin as he stood and hugged her silently.

'Emily, darling.' He reached for her and kissed the top of her head. 'Why don't we tell Linda our own exciting news?'

Linda looked between them, her eyes wide with anticipation.

'What is it?'

Damien held Emily close to him as he announced, 'We are having a baby. It was officially confirmed this morning.'

'Oh, Emily, how wonderful.' Linda enveloped her in a crushing hug. 'It wasn't a stomach bug after all!'

'No.' Emily smiled. 'But for the next seven and a half months don't let anyone come near me with an oyster. I just couldn't bear it.'

Damien and Linda laughed and then, excusing herself, Linda left to return to Rose's side. Damien looked down at Emily and, reaching inside his pocket said, 'I forgot to tell you, darling.' He took out the cheque she'd given to his brother. 'This cheque has been cancelled.'

'Cancelled?' She looked at the slip of paper in puzzlement.

'Yes.'

'You mean I haven't lost all my money? Danny didn't use it?'

'No, he didn't.' He reached into his pocket again and handed her another document.

'What is it?'

'The title deeds to your apartment. I was the impatient buyer.'

She stared at him in amazement. 'You bought it?'

'I thought we should keep it in the family,' he said. 'Who knows? One day one of our kids might need an apartment. I was thinking ahead.'

'I don't know what to say.' Her eyes misted over.

'You don't need to say anything.'

'I love you.'

'Except perhaps that—every single day for the rest of our lives, OK?' He smiled down at her.

Emily's eyes danced with merriment as she lifted her mouth to his.

'It's a deal.'

Modern Romance™
...seduction and passion guaranteed

Tender Romance™
...love affairs that last a lifetime

Medical Romance™
...medical drama on the pulse

Historical Romance™
...rich, vivid and passionate

Sensual Romance™
...sassy, sexy and seductive

Blaze Romance™
...the temperature's rising

27 new titles every month.

Live the emotion

MILLS & BOON

MILLS & BOON

Live the emotion

Modern Romance™

SOLD TO THE SHEIKH by Miranda Lee

When supermodel Charmaine donates herself as a prize at a charity auction, she is amazed to discover the winning bidder is Prince Ali of Dubar, the same arrogant Arab sheikh she rejected a year ago! Her amazement turns to shock when Prince Ali makes her an outrageous offer...

HIS INHERITED BRIDE by Jacqueline Baird

Julia has rushed to Chile to see if an inheritance will give her the much needed money required to help her mother. But in order to claim a thing she must marry gorgeous Italian Randolfo Carducci! Multimillionaire Rand can give Julia anything she desires...but on *his* terms.

THE BEDROOM BARTER by Sara Craven

Chellie Greer is penniless and without her passport, stuck working in a seedy club with no means of escape. And then Ash Brennan walks in. What's such a powerful, irresistible stranger doing in a place like this? Ash offers her a way out – but Chellie has to wonder why...

THE SICILIAN SURRENDER by Sandra Marton

When it comes to women, rich and powerful Stefano Lucchesi has known them – except Fallon O'Connell. Beautiful and wealthy, she needs no one – least of all Stefano. Then an accident ends her career. Now she needs Stefano's help – even if that means surrender...

On sale 6th February 2004

Available at most branches of WHSmith, Tesco, Martins, Borders, Eason, Sainsbury's and all good paperback bookshops.

MILLS & BOON®

Live the emotion

Modern Romance™

McGILLIVRAY'S MISTRESS by Anne McAllister

Fiona Dunbar isn't ready for the return of Lachlan McGillivray to Pelican Cay. His roguish reputation goes before him, and soon the whole island is certain they are having an affair! But Fiona wants to live life on her own terms. If Lachlan wants her he'll have to make her his bride!

THE TYCOON'S VIRGIN BRIDE by Sandra Field

Twelve years ago, Jenessa's secret infatuation with tycoon Bryce Laribee turned to passion — but when he discovered she was a virgin he walked out! Now, the attraction between them is just as intense, and Bryce is determined to finish what they started. But Jenessa has a secret or two...

THE ITALIAN'S TOKEN WIFE by Julia James

Furious at his father, Italian millionaire Rafaello di Viscenti vows to marry the first woman he sees — Magda, a single mother desperately trying to make ends meet by doing his cleaning! Rafaello's proposal comes with a financial reward, so Magda has no choice but to accept...

A SPANISH ENGAGEMENT by Kathryn Ross

The future of Carrie Michaels' orphaned niece is threatened and there is only one answer: find a man and pretend she's engaged! Carrie can't believe her luck when sexy Spanish lawyer Max Santos offers to help — but little does she realise that Max has needs of his own...

On sale 6th February 2004

Available at most branches of WHSmith, Tesco, Martins, Borders, Eason, Sainsbury's and all good paperback bookshops.

MillsandBoon.co.uk

books | authors | online reads | magazine | membership

Visit millsandboon.co.uk and discover your one-stop shop for romance!

Find out everything you want to know about romance novels in one place. Read about and buy our novels online anytime you want.

* Choose and buy books from an extensive selection of Mills & Boon® titles.

* Enjoy top authors and *New York Times* best-selling authors – from Penny Jordan and Miranda Lee to Sandra Marton and Nicola Cornick!

* Take advantage of our amazing **FREE** book offers.

* In our Authors' area find titles currently available from all your favourite authors.

* Get hooked on one of our fabulous online reads, with new chapters updated weekly.

* Check out the fascinating articles in our magazine section.

Visit us online at
www.millsandboon.co.uk

…you'll want to come back again and again!!

4 FREE

books and a surprise gift!

We would like to take this opportunity to thank you for reading this Mills & Boon® book by offering you the chance to take FOUR more specially selected titles from the Modern Romance™ series absolutely FREE! We're also making this offer to introduce you to the benefits of the Reader Service™—

- ★ FREE home delivery
- ★ FREE gifts and competitions
- ★ FREE monthly Newsletter
- ★ Exclusive Reader Service offers
- ★ Books available before they're in the shops

Accepting these FREE books and gift places you under no obligation to buy, you may cancel at any time, even after receiving your free shipment. Simply complete your details below and return the entire page to the address below. *You don't even need a stamp!*

YES! Please send me 4 free Modern Romance books and a surprise gift. I understand that unless you hear from me, I will receive 6 superb new titles every month for just £2.60 each, postage and packing free. I am under no obligation to purchase any books and may cancel my subscription at any time. The free books and gift will be mine to keep in any case.

P4ZED

Ms/Mrs/Miss/Mr ....Initials........................
BLOCK CAPITALS PLEASE

Surname ....

Address ....

....

....Postcode.................

Send this whole page to:
UK: FREEPOST CN81, Croydon, CR9 3WZ
EIRE: PO Box 4546, Kilcock, County Kildare (stamp required)

Offer valid in UK and Eire only and not available to current Reader Service subscribers to this series. We reserve the right to refuse an application and applicants must be aged 18 years or over. Only one application per household. Terms and prices subject to change without notice. Offer expires 30th April 2004. As a result of this application, you may receive offers from Harlequin Mills & Boon and other carefully selected companies. If you would prefer not to share in this opportunity please write to The Data Manager at the address above.

Mills & Boon® is a registered trademark owned by Harlequin Mills & Boon Limited.
Modern Romance™ is being used as a trademark.
The Reader Service™ is being used as a trademark.